Bruce E. Arrington

Every Perfect Gift
The Original Screenplay

Paisley

Every Perfect Gift

Ebook ISBN 978-1-942031-15-4
Print ISBN 978-1-942031-20-8

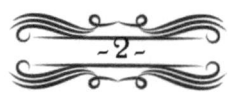

INT. WOOD SHOP – HOLMES COUNTY, OHIO –2038

We see a wood shop akin to centuries past, with three bed frames in various stages of completion. Stools, chairs and parts of other unfinished furnishings stack floor to ceiling. Fine craftsman tools display neatly along dark stained walls. Pneumatic drills, sander and drill press display on the far wall.

JACOB MILLER, early 50s, stout and greying; SAMUEL, 17, tall and wiry, brown hair. Both in aprons, simple shirts and pants, held by with suspenders. They polish a dining room table.

> JACOB
>
> This will look good in their kitchen, don't you think?

> SAMUEL
>
> (*long yawn*)
>
> It is a fine gift,
> Father.

> JACOB
>
> Do you need to rest before we go?

> SAMUEL
>
> (*flushes*)
>
> I'm all right. I just didn't sleep well last night. I am sorry if you were wakened.

Jacob shrugs, his eyes showing the concern his shoulders don't.

> JACOB
>
> I don't know what to tell you anymore. When you were a little boy I thought your dreams would fade. They just seemed too fantastic to believe.
>
> (*hesitates*)

But I do think the Beilers are looking forward to the delivery!

They carefully maneuver the table out of the shop.

EXT. WOOD SHOP -- DAY

FADE UP TITLE:

HOLMES COUNTY, OHIO

MONDAY, OCTOBER 18, 2038

Red, orange, and yellow maple leaves drift from giant trees, dance in the wind, and finally fall slowly to the ground.
GABRIEL, an aging black Standardbred horse, waits hitched to a black wagon, tail twitching and head rubbing against his leg.
Jacob and Samuel load the table onto the wagon. They climb in and Jacob takes the reins.

JACOB

Gabriel.

Gabriel lumbers down the road.

EXT. ROAD – MID MORNING

Samuel briefly looks sideways at his father. Jacob stares off into the nearby patch of rows upon rows of large orange pumpkins.

JACOB
Last week Daniel turned 18?

SAMUEL
(*swallows*)

Yes.

JACOB
(*shoulders droop*)
They will come for him soon.

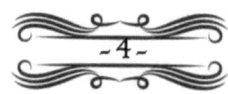

SAMUEL

I know. I hope they will forget and leave him
alone.

JACOB

Maybe that will happen. He's
their only child.

SAMUEL
(*face tightens*)

Maybe.

EXT. BEILER HOME – DAY

*A yellow and white farmhouse stands proudly, with a yard filled with tall
cottonwood trees, swaying gently in the fall breeze. Jacob and Samuel greet
DAVID BEILER, late 40's, built, dark brown hair; his wife ANNA, late
40's, sturdy, blonde hair; and son DANIEL, 18, stout, light blonde. All
three are dressed in Amish garb.*

DAVID
(*grinning*)
Your timing is perfect, Jacob.

ANNA

The leg broke off again. We ate breakfast on the floor!

*Jacob and David laugh. Samuel and Daniel carry the table inside the
house. The parents follow.*

EXT. BEILER HOME – MOMENTS LATER

*Samuel and Daniel run out of the house with baseball gear. They sprint to
a nearby mowed field. Samuel wins by an inch.
Samuel and Daniel toss a ball back and forth. Daniel's throws are intense.*

DANIEL
So tell me, Samuel. How is
Katie?

Samuel pauses after catching the ball. He shrugs with a slight smile.

SAMUEL

Don't know. Haven't seen her.

DANIEL

(*teasing*)

She wrote me.

SAMUEL

(*surprised*)

She wrote you? Why?

DANIEL

Birthday card. She lives in Kent. Did you know that?

Samuel nods.

DANIEL

I wonder what she is doing there.

SAMUEL

You always wonder about my sister!

DANIEL

Yes. I do.

EXT. FIELD--AFTERNOON

Samuel hits a fly ball to Daniel. As Daniel backs up to catch, his attention is suddenly drawn elsewhere. Face paling, his arms hang limp. The ball lands on his right with a thud.

DANIEL

I waited too long.

Samuel turns to see a dust cloud rising in the air a half mile away. A vehicle appears -- a futuristic-looking army jeep! Daniel drops his glove as Samuel joins him.

SAMUEL

I thought you said-

> DANIEL
> (*yells*)

You know you're next!

The army jeep tears into the Beiler's yard. Two armed SOLDIERS dressed in black fatigues, hop out, hurry to the front door and bang on it.

> SAMUEL

Daniel...what are you going to do?

> DANIEL
> (*freaked*)

Leave. Now!

Daniel turns and bolts. Samuel, wide-eyed, tries to keep up.

EXT. MAPLE FOREST—AFTERNOON

Half naked sugar maple trees with their and yellow and orange leaves sway in the wind. Daniel is bent over behind a small cluster of trees, breathing hard. Samuel catches up.

> DANIEL
> (*panicked*)

Joshua did nothing. He didn't...he didn't say no. He just went with them! And now...and now he's dead!

Samuel turns to see the jeep heading straight at them.

> SAMUEL
> (*pleading*)

Hide! Live with us!

DANIEL

Hide where? They still don't know what I look
like. Run! They'll chase you so I can get away.
Go...now!

*Samuel takes off, out of the woods and onto a
large field —full speed.*

EXT. FIELD – AFTERNOON

*The military jeep roars in its approach and overtakes Samuel, who stops up
short. It circles and blocks his path.*

*SERGEANT HADEN, early thirties, built like a linebacker, with a
premium cigar in mouth, jumps out of the jeep and gets in Samuel's face.
He's ticked.*

HADEN

You know why I hate my job so much, Beiler?
Do you?

Samuel stares at the ground, frozen.

HADEN

Because this is what I get to do every stinkin' day:
chase you Amish all over this god-forsaken
country. Most drafted recruits realize their duty
and report in! But not you. Oh no! You run and
hide, thinking we'll never find you, or that we'll
forget your name or where you live or that you
were even drafted in the first place!

*Haden spits and shakes his head. He grabs some black army fatigues
from the jeep and drops them to the ground.*

HADEN

Well, you know what, Beiler? You screwed up
my schedule. Because you're late reporting in, I'm
late taking you in. Because I'm late taking you in,
other recruits are late reporting in. So my

commanding officer looks bad. I look bad. The other recruits look bad and you look bad. So we're going to do this right here. Take off your clothes.

SAMUEL
(*shocked*)
Take off my clothes?

HADEN
(*in Samuel's face*)
You expect to go to boot camp looking like a blue tart?
(*points down*)
Here. Fatigues. My men will cut your girlie locks, and let you say good-bye to your mommy and daddy. Then we go to boot camp and make a real man out of you. Now, Beiler, strip!

SAMUEL
(*evenly, enjoying this*)
My name isn't Beiler. It's Miller.

Haden scans Samuel without flinching. He snaps his fingers at the other soldier.
HADEN
Miller? Don't we have a Miller coming up soon?

The soldier grabs a clipboard.
SOLDIER
Yes sergeant, Samuel Miller. Eighteenth birthday on November 18.

Haden smiles. He puffs his cigar in Samuel's face.

HADEN

Well then, *Samuel Miller,* I guess you're free to
go. For now. But don't think I'll forget this little
prank of yours.
(*turns his head*)
And that must be Daniel Beiler! Load up boys!

We see Daniel running away with another jeep closing in.

HADEN
(*contempt*)
I look forward to working with you *real* soon,
Samuel Miller.

Haden snatches the fatigues, jumps in the jeep and the driver spins away.

EXT. BEILER HOME -- AFTERNOON

Samuel nears Daniel's house, shoulders drooped, eyes down.
Day is overcast. Two military jeeps fly by Samuel. They have Daniel.
Daniel, in army fatigues and a buzz haircut, leaps out of the jeep and
jogs into the house. David, Anna and Samuel follow.

HADEN

Ten minutes Beiler!

INT. DANIEL'S BEDROOM --MINUTES LATER

A simple room, consisting of a bed, chair, small brown table, lamp and
white dresser. Daniel throws a ratty suitcase on his bed and starts packing.
His face is beet red. He looks mad, really mad! David and Anna stare at
their son, distraught, helpless.

DANIEL
(*controlled*)
Father, mother. I will see you in a few minutes.

David and Anna hesitate and leave.

> SAMUEL
>
> I was hoping they would forget. Wouldn't come.

Daniel hurriedly stuffs a few last pieces of his clothing into the suitcase and latches it closed. One latch pops open twice before finally holding in place.
Daniel looks to the floor, then at Samuel.

> DANIEL
>
> Forget your dreams, Samuel. Leave before it's too late.
>
> (*pause*)
>
> Everyone says it's nice in Canada.

Daniel grabs his suitcase and heads for the door.

EXT. BEILER HOME –DAY

Daniel hugs his father and kisses his mother. A mist forms in her eyes. Daniel climbs into the jeep, luggage in hand. Haden roughly jerks him into the back seat.

Anna reaches out to him. David gently restrains her. Anna cries quietly in protest.
Daniel looks at Samuel and gives half-hearted wave. Samuel waves back. The jeep screams down the road. Jacob puts his arm around Samuel as everyone's eyes follow the dust trail.

EXT. ROAD – LATE AFTERNOON

Black clouds circle in the sky. The wind howls.
Jacob pulls on the reins and Gabriel stops. Daniel's old clothes and shoes lay scattered on the ground, tattered and dirty. After Samuel retrieves them, Jacob places his arm around Samuel's shoulders.

> JACOB
>
> I am sorry Samuel.
>
> (*quietly*)
>
> Gabriel.

Gabriel slowly ambers down the road.

INT. WAGON – EVENING

A dark, windy rainstorm drench father, son and horse. Lightning flashes in the distance as they continue toward home, man and teen huddled together.

INT. MILLER KITCHEN – NIGHT

The kitchen is simple though spacious, with an ice box, wood stove, and handsome kitchen table with five chairs, decorated with an Amaryllis. Jacob and Samuel eat fried meat, pasta and bread. Both are wrapped in blankets. Samuel's mother REBECCA, severe, early 50s, stares at them.

Samuel yawns after he finishes. He kisses his mother and father on the forehead and leaves the kitchen.

Jacob and Rebecca stare at each other. Rebecca's chin trembles.

INT. SAMUEL'S BEDROOM –NIGHT

We see a clean and tidy bedroom. Samuel sits on his twin bed next to a lampstand. By the light of his lamp he reads his tattered draft notice. He hesitates a few seconds, then crumples it up and throws it against the opposite wall. He lays down and stares at the ceiling, fists clenched. But almost at once he closes his eyes and falls asleep. Samuel tosses and turns. We hear sounds of jets, helicopters, noises of gun fire, screams of men and women.

After another moment of dream violence, Samuel jerks up in his bed.

SAMUEL

Aauuugggh!

His father appears with a lantern.

> JACOB
>
> Samuel! Are you all right?

> SAMUEL
> (*breathing hard*)
>
> The dream...it's growing.

> JACOB
> (*alarmed*)
>
> Growing? What do you mean?

> SAMUEL
> (*pauses*)
>
> I have to go, father. I have to save
> him...somehow.

> JACOB
>
> But what about the soldiers? What if they find
> you? What if you are caught?

> SAMUEL
> (*eyes pleading*)
>
> I have to try.

> JACOB
>
> We will talk. Tomorrow...we will talk.

INT. KITCHEN – MORNING

Jacob, Rebecca, and Samuel sit around the table, eating a breakfast casserole. Samuel stares at the two empty chairs. Rebecca cries silently until Jacob takes her hand.

> REBECCA
> (*softly*)
>
> Why is God taking away our children?

Jacob pats Rebecca's hand.

JACOB

Others in our community have suffered too,
Rebecca. We must trust God.

REBECCA

When Amos was drafted you said we must trust
God. When Katie left you said that God knows
best.

JACOB

God's ways are higher than our ways.
His thoughts are higher than our thoughts.

SAMUEL

Don't worry mother. I will be all right.

REBECCA
(*worried*)
And where will you live? What will you do?
Where will you go to church and worship God?

JACOB

I will go into town and call Katie. He can stay
with her.

REBECCA

And what will we tell the soldiers when they
come for Samuel? And who will do Samuel's
work? You cannot make furniture all by yourself
anymore, Jacob.

JACOB

Cousin John said he was looking for work.

EXT. GRANDMOTHER PRISCILLA'S
HOUSE – MID MORNING

This tall 'grandfather' house stands next to the back side of Samuel's home. Samuel knocks on the door. PRISCILLA, his frail and small grandmother, with snow-white wispy hair, slowly opens the door and smiles at him. Age spots cover her face. Her spectacles are halfway down her nose.

SAMUEL

(*depressed*)

Hello grandmother.

PRISCILLA

Samuel.

Samuel walks inside, slowly, uncertainly.

INT. LIVING ROOM – DAY

In the sparsely furnished home several black hats hang, lined up along a wall.
Samuel slumps down on an old brown couch. Priscilla trots off to the kitchen.

PRISCILLA (O.S.)

You leave tomorrow?

Samuel nods, looking wide-eyed at the floor.

PRISCILLA (O.S.)

You know, Samuel, going away could be a good thing for you.

SAMUEL

(*wrinkles nose*)

What do you mean, grandmother? How could this be good?

PRISCILLA

(O.S.)

Oh...well, you will be able to see Katie again. Perhaps meet up with your brother. See what the world is really like. Fall in love, maybe.

SAMUEL

But grandmother, I belong here, not out there. I don't want to see the world. I was to be baptized next week. And this...this dream keeps haunting me. Fall in love? Out there?

Priscilla hands Samuel a cup of hot chocolate.

PRISCILLA
I was once 'out there'. There are plenty of places to see in this world. Some may surprise you with their beauty.

Samuel gulps down his drink and stares at the hats on the wall. Priscilla takes a black Stetson hat and holds it gingerly. It looks good as new.

PRISCILLA
Isaac bought this when we first moved here. It became his favorite hat. He had a dream to raise a family to love God, to be part of something so important. And he was. But he had to leave his world of comfort and security. His dream was worth everything to him.
(*pause*)
Samuel, don't let anything stand in the way of your dreams.

SAMUEL
My dreams? Grandmother, I don't. I don't even understand these dreams! I don't really even want them.

PRISCILLA
Samuel, ever since you were six years old these dreams have been a part of who you are, a sign of what God wants you to do. Now, you can choose to accept them as his gift or fight them.
(*pause*)

Your grandfather would want you to have this.

Priscilla holds out the hat. Samuel accepts it gingerly as his eyes moisten.

> SAMUEL
>
> I still miss him. He could guide me if he was still here.
>
> PRISCILLA
>
> I think you already know what you should do, Samuel. You just need to make up your mind and do it.

Samuel tries on the hat. Still a little too big.

EXT. WALNUT CREEK BUS STOP —MORNING
A simple rut-filled dirt turnoff with a small ticket booth contrasts sharply with a parked futuristic-looking travel bus, sleek and streamlined. Samuel carries an old suitcase, a backpack and bus ticket.
Rebecca hugs and kisses him.
Samuel stoops as Priscilla pulls him in and hugs him tightly.

> PRISCILLA
>
> Remember, God has a good plan for you. A good plan. He will take care of you and bring you back to us.

Samuel looks down at her. A drawn out worried smile.
Jacob shakes Samuel's hand and passes him a small package.

> JACOB
>
> Have a good birthday, son.
>
> SAMUEL
>
> I will.
>
> JACOB
>
> You have your papers?

Samuel nods. Tears build in his eyes. He looks down.

> JACOB
>
> Good. If things don't work out, Ontario is a fine
> place to raise a family. You are now your own
> man.

Jacob hugs Samuel tightly, then turns away.
Samuel looks longingly at his family once more. He turns and climbs
onto the bus.

INT. BUS – MID-MORNING

As Samuel climbs inside, he notices there is no driver and no driver seat.
A computer console asks for his ticket and sucks it up instantly. It tells
him to which seat he is assigned. Samuel moves three quarters down the
aisle, looks out a window and waves to his family as he sits.

Samuel's haunted face stares at his father and mother as the bus takes off
by itself. His eyes tell all:

I'm alone.
I'm afraid.
I don't want to be here.

INT. BUS – LATE MORNING

Samuel is slunk down in his seat. He opens the gift from his father to reveal
a new German Bible and $1000 cash. He looks up at the large screen TV
three rows ahead of him to see a Kent State University ad.

An ambulance screams by. Samuel jumps.

Loud sirens wail behind the bus. Samuel turns to see a supersized military
jeep flashing its lights. Samuel sinks in his seat and pales. Loosens his collar.

The bus stops and the door opens.
An armed MP wearing a black uniform and helmet boards.

> MP
>
> Miller?

Samuel shuts his eyes, sighs and shakes his head.

> MP
>
> Joshua Miller?

A short-haired MAN, 20s, on Samuel's right, leaps up against a window. He grabs and opens the emergency exit handles. Jumps out. The MP flies off the bus. Samuel looks out the window. Joshua Miller lays flat on his stomach, handcuffed and being read his rights.

Samuel sinks back down in his seat, eyes closed, trying to steady his breathing. After a moment the bus takes off again.

EXT. BUS STOP, KENT – AFTERNOON

We see nicely paved parking lots, dozens of new cars and several buses loading and off-loading PASSENGERS.
Samuel's older sister KATIE, 21, shorter by six inches but with the same brown hair, waves to him as he exits the bus. They embrace.

> KATIE
> (*laughs*)
>
> I can't believe how much you have grown! Little brother!

Samuel grabs his luggage and hands Katie his backpack.

> KATIE
>
> Father said you were having your dreams again. And needed to leave?

> SAMUEL
> (*hesitates*)
>
> Something like that.

Katie studies Samuel.

> KATIE
>
> You can talk to me Samuel. You know that.

> SAMUEL

I know, Katie.

A beat.

> SAMUEL
> (*reassuring smile*)

I know.

Katie leads him to her cherried-out, yellow Mazda Miata convertible. Samuel stares at the beautiful car. He glances at Katie and then again at the car. The very small car.

> KATIE
> (*beams*)

My baby. Got it last year for only 46. Only ten years old with a hundred thousand. And it's fast. Real fast.

> SAMUEL
> (*shakes head*)

You paid $46,000 for a car?

> KATIE

Yep. Comes fully loaded: automated GIS computer navigation, an autopilot system, the works. Let's go!

Samuel carefully slides in. Three sets of buckles wrap around him. He grabs his seat and licks his lips.

> SAMUEL

This is death on four small wheels.

EXT. E. SUMMIT STREET -- DAY

The Miata speeds east.

INT. MIATA –DAY

Samuel's eyes are saucer-size. His white knuckles hold on the grips for dear life.
Katie throws a look his way and slows way down. She turns on a public radio station.

> NEWSCASTER (V.O.)
> ...latest surveys show an increase of 50 cents over the past week. The national average is now $19.17 a gallon for gasoline. In related news, experts have determined that within five years the world's remaining oil supply will be exhausted, due to significant increases in almost every country of the world.

> KATIE
> (*sighs, turns off radio*)
> Great. I'll still owe with nowhere to go. Stupid idiots.

> SAMUEL
> What idiots?

> KATIE
> Take your pick, Samuel...our nearsighted, narrow-minded, bigoted, warmonger President for one.

> SAMUEL
> (*glares*)
> You shouldn't say that. He is the President.

> KATIE
> (Sotto voce)
> Dictator from Hades is more like it.
> (*pause, fake smile*)
> So how are things at home? Anyone miss me?

> SAMUEL
> Of course you are missed. How can you ask that?

KATIE

Well, do father or mother ever talk about me? Or Amos?

SAMUEL

Not really, but on your birthday they're always depressed.

(*pause*)

So...do you ever miss the community?

KATIE

(*shrugs*)

No. I keep busy. I'm a part time student here at Kent State, and I work at the Parks and Rec.

SAMUEL
Parks and Rec?

KATIE

You know, *parks*. Places where people go and get away from city life. And speaking of *city life*, now that you'll be staying with me, you'll need to learn how to use certain...things.

Katie grins.

SAMUEL

I know. Father told me about your lights and stoves and refrigerators...

KATIE
And television...shower...toilet. Telephones.

SAMUEL

(*mouth slackens*)
Telephone? You have a telephone?

KATIE

(*laughs, nods*)
Yes! I have a landline and a cell phone!

EXT. KATIE'S HOUSE – DAY

The Miata sweeps up to a small, grey, one bedroom house. The mailbox reads 'I533 Chadwick Road'.

INT. HOUSE -- DAY

The house comes with standard but aging appliances. An old dining table and orange Hide-a-bed couch stick out, way oversized for the tiny space. A 70-inch TV sits along a wall.

Samuel runs his hand over the dining table. He scans the couch to find three pair of jeans and four colored t-shirts.

> KATIE
>
> Have to sleep on the Hide-A-Bed...sorry.

> SAMUEL
> (*shrugs*)
>
> Not a problem.

> KATIE
> (*gestures*)
>
> Some clothes... the TV...these for the lights, and I have a surprise for you.

INT. BATHROOM –DAY

Katie points to the toilet with laser sensors. Samuel rolls his eyes.

> KATIE
>
> No outhouse here, brother. Just step away and it's taken care of. Or you can talk to it.

> SAMUEL
> (*openly staring*)
>
> Talk to a toilet?

> KATIE

Yes, say *flush*. Don't roll your eyes, it works.

Katie opens the shower stall and points to six buttons with temp labels.

> KATIE
> Hot, cold, you'll figure it out.

> SAMUEL
> We have showers at home.

> KATIE
> (*smirks*)
> Not this kind.
> (*pause*)
> Well go ahead and try it. You stink like Gabriel!

Katie leaves.

INT. SHOWER STALL -- DAY

Samuel stares at the buttons, ready for a shower.

> SAMUEL
> (*sneers*)
> We don't use hot water at home.

He pushes the cold water button.

INT. HALLWAY –DAY

Katie listens to Samuel scream. She smiles in satisfaction and walks away humming.

INT. SHOWER STALL -- DAY

The water is off except for a few drops falling off the shower head. Samuel stares at the buttons, wide-eyed, breathing heavily. He shivers violently.

INT. LIVING ROOM –AFTERNOON

Samuel and Katie sit on the couch, watching the news.

> ANCHOR WOMAN
>
> After President Stone narrowly won his second term last year, he has been campaigning almost non-stop to convince members of Congress to pass a law abolishing Presidential term limits. It looks like he will finally get his wish as the Senate approved Bill S2020-45 this morning. More after this.

> KATIE
>
> Oh perfect. Now we'll never get rid of him.

A Mazda commercial appears. Holographic Miata images suddenly appear in the living room, 3D.

> KATIE
> (*triumphant*)
> See? Best car in the world.

Samuel rolls eyes and snorts. But he is curious about the holographic image.

> SAMUEL
> How do they do that?

The news returns.

> ANCHOR WOMAN
>
> In light of the recent terrorist threats against the United States, the President has received expanded powers from Congress. This includes indefinite draft authority, the shared right to declare war, and increased domestic spying. The President and congressional leaders have been quoted as saying they still need to work out the details.

> KATIE
> (*deadpan*)

Uh-huh.

> ANCHOR WOMAN

In other news, twenty thousand protesters marched on Washington today after President Stone unveiled his plans to control the world's remaining oil supply, in his words, "seeking to protect America's interests above all else." Fifteen protesters were shot-

Katie flicks off the TV.

> KATIE

Great. Just one more reason for everyone to hate us.

> (*to Samuel*)

So this is the guy you're supposed to save? This...this terrorist?

Katie walks off to the kitchen. Samuel grabs the remote and flicks the TV back on, changing channels. A 3-D commercial for Kent State University comes on.

> SAMUEL
> (*awed*)

Television is...so cool.

INT. LIVING ROOM – NIGHT

Samuel relaxes on the couch, staring at one of his drawings. Katie sits by him, peering at the picture: a dark portal.

> KATIE

What is it?

> SAMUEL

The corridor.

KATIE

Oh yeah. From your dream?

(*pause*)

Hey. You should be proud of me—last month I
went to an open session on worm holes.

SAMUEL

(*suddenly excited*)

Worm holes? Here?

KATIE

Yep. NASA is now sending their probes through
worm holes. Some guy named Cameron gave a
talk at Smith Hall, which has a great planetarium
you ought to check out.

Samuel's brow rises.

KATIE

By the way, since you're still under 18 you can
audit any class this semester for free.

SAMUEL

(*smirk*)

Real science classes?

KATIE

They won't give you the books, but the library
should have what you need. If you want,
tomorrow we'll sign you up.

*Katie grabs her backpack, pulls out a Kent State catalog and hands it to
Samuel.*

KATIE

Pick out your classes. Bring your birth certificate
and tell them you're Amish. Oh...one more thing.

                    SAMUEL
                   (*distracted*)

Hmm?

                    KATIE

Remember to use words like 'please' and 'thank
you'. It will help you out here in the English
world.

                    SAMUEL
                    (*snaps*)

I'm not rude.

                    KATIE
                   (*deadpan*)

Never said you were. Good night, Samuel!

Katie leaves the room.

                    SAMUEL

All right...thank you.

Samuel studies the catalog. A wide smile forms.

EXT. MICHAEL SCHWARTZ CENTER – DAY

*Samuel, now dressed in jeans and a red t-shirt with KSU in black bold
letters, pores over his class schedule as scores of students breeze past. Katie
looks over his shoulder.*

                    SAMUEL
                   (*pleased*)

Applied physics, electrical engineering, advanced
quantum physics, relativity theory and wormhole
studies. Everything I wanted!

KATIE

Don't you think you overdid it?

Samuel shakes his head.

SAMUEL

I already know some of this.

KATIE

(*smirk*)

Yeah, I believe you. All those trips to the library. How could I forget?

SAMUEL

(*gleeful*)

I remember the romance novel you tried to check out!

KATIE

(*eyes flash*)

So does everyone else. One of the reasons I left. Why are you using your middle name?

SAMUEL

I think it sounds more...distinctive. Physics started at 8:30. Where is Smith Hall?

KATIE

(*points east*)

This way, Levi.

EXT. SMITH HALL – DAY

Samuel waves to Katie as he enters the large, proud building.

INT. PHYSICS LECTURE ROOM -- DAY

The clock on the wall reads 8:43.

A half-filled class of STUDENTS is seated, most of them whispering or snoozing as the advanced quantum physics PROFESSOR lectures. Samuel takes a seat halfway down the right side of the aisle. Several students stare at him with bemused faces.

INT. LECTURE ROOM – 45 MINUTES LATER

Samuel waits as the students leave the room. Another STUDENT, Jarrod, early 20's, athletic, walks up, offers his hand.

> JARROD
> Name's Jarrod. I saw you come in a few minutes late. And don't worry, you didn't miss anything. So...you like physics? Or are you lost?

> SAMUEL
> *(shrugs, takes his hand)*
> It's not that bad.

> JARROD
> You really understand all that stuff?

Samuel shrugs.

> JARROD
> I get it. You're one of those gifted students. Finished high school at age 12?

> SAMUEL
> I finished school when I was 14.

Two other STUDENTS, Jarrod's age, walk up.

> JARROD
> Hey guys, this is ---

                    SAMUEL

Samuel.

                    JARROD

Probably the youngest quantum physics genius in
school!
                    (*laughs*)
This is Cameron and Hillary.

*Samuel looks at Cameron: handsome, tall, early 20s. Hillary,
strawberry blonde and same age, holds onto his arm.*

                    SAMUEL

You gave the worm holes lecture?

Cameron brightens. Straightens.

                    CAMERON

See guys, another fan!

                    SAMUEL

I didn't see it. My sister told me about it.

                    CAMERON
                    (*smile fades*)

Oh.

                    HILLARY

So...you're a student?

                    SAMUEL
                    (*shakes head*)

Just auditing some classes.

                    CAMERON
                    (*loses interest*)

Later Sam.

The three friends take off. Samuel glares at Cameron.

> SAMUEL
>
> My name is Samuel.

EXT. OBSERVATORY – A WEEK LATER

A huge white observatory dwarfs the two attached buildings.
A sign on the door reads: "Funding for this Observatory provided by
NASA, Kent State University and your local tax dollars."
Samuel opens the door and walks inside.

INT. OBSERVATORY HALL -- DAY

Samuel sees Jarrod and waves.

> JARROD
>
> Hey, Sam, right? What's up?

> SAMUEL
> (*swallows his annoyance*)
> Samuel. Hey Jarrod. My sister told me to check
> this place out.

> JARROD
> Come on, I'll give you the ten dollar tour.
> (*pause*)
> So how are your classes coming along?

> SAMUEL
> (*hesitates*)
> They're okay, but not much help for my project.
Jarrod stops mid-stride.

> JARROD
> You mean like a senior project?

INT. OBSERVATORY STUDY ROOM—DAY

A star-chart mural covers the ceiling. Antique telescopes decorate the room. Cameron and Hillary, side by side, pore over a star map.

> HILLARY
> (*gently, pointing to a chart*)

Right there.

> CAMERON
> (*laughing, gentle*)

No, babe, over there. I -

> JARROD

Hey Cameron. Samuel needs help with *space travel.* Got a minute?

> CAMERON
> (*humored*)

Sure. Let's uhhh…take a look.

Samuel hands his drawing and notes to Cameron, who grins at first. But soon his face hardens. Hillary and Jarrod look over Cameron's shoulder.

> CAMERON

You are really trying to travel through space?

> SAMUEL

To other countries.

Cameron takes his cell phone out and dials. We hear someone pick up.

> CAMERON

Hey Dad.

INT. OBSERVATORY STUDY ROOM – NIGHT

Samuel, Cameron, Jarrod and Hillary sit around a table. Samuel's notes are spread out revealing diagrams and calculations.

> CAMERON
>
> So, it's all set. Tomorrow night we meet at Sam's place. And with my dad's background at the Glenn Research Lab, this might really go somewhere.

> JARROD
>
> You could make a fortune!

> SAMUEL
>
> I don't care about the money. I don't want to sell it.

> CAMERON
>
> You're kidding, right? I mean, if this all proves out, it could lead to a huge industry almost overnight! You'd be rich.

> JARROD
>
> Yeah, think about it, Samuel! You could make out like crazy! What, you don't like money?

Samuel shrugs with a deadpan expression.

> HILLARY
>
> All right guys. Don't worry about money. Right now let's just think about how we get it done.

> CAMERON
> (*ecstatic!*)
> Think of all the possibilities! Instant travel!

> JARROD

A free trip to Jamaica, Hawaii, anywhere!

INT. KATIE'S HOUSE – NIGHT

KYLE ABRAHAM, Cameron's father, sits next to Samuel reading the drawings and notes. Kyle wears a threadbare suit. He's balding, mid-50s, energetic.

KYLE

This is amazing, Samuel. Your work looks very solid.

CAMERON

So what's the next step?

JARROD

We launch the project! We make it work!

HILLARY
(*perturbed*)

What? With no money?

KYLE
(*confident*)

A budget shortfall caused Research I Lab to close last month, but I'll talk to President Hachmann. He might let us use it. The computers and equipment belong to the University, but we—I mean you, Samuel, can still claim all rights to the project. I can take care of that for you.

CAMERON
(*snaps his fingers*)

Hey, what about Adara Jacinto? She's super rich and likes to invest in these types of projects. She was always raving about your wormhole project, Dad.

KYLE
(*nods proudly*)
Good point. I'll call her tomorrow.

SAMUEL
(*clears throat*)
I just want to make sure that this
is never used as a weapon of war.

A beat.

KYLE
(*serious*)
I couldn't agree more, Samuel. And it's
imperative we keep it away from people like our
president that would only use it to destroy—

CAMERON
(*flushing*)
Dad.

KYLE
Anyway, I belong to a society whose sole purpose
is to promote peace, in all countries of the world.
This is a noble effort to promote scientific
research and discovery.
(*emotional*)
So Samuel, back to your notes...

INT. KITCHEN – LATE NIGHT

*Samuel and Katie sit at the table. Samuel pores over his notes. Katie's arms
cross and she stares at her brother.*

KATIE

So...when are you going to tell them who this is really for?

SAMUEL

They don't need to know. They might think I'm crazy.

KATIE

You're right. They probably would. Did you hear the latest? Stone is sending 100 nuclear missiles overseas. He is building silos at our bases in case we need to knock off a few more countries.

SAMUEL

(*irritated*)

Whatever.

Katie slaps both palms on the table. Samuel jumps in response.

KATIE

(*flushed*)

Samuel!

(*pause*)

Saving him might mean the END Of THE WORLD. Did you ever stop to think about that?

SAMUEL

(*defensive*)

Of course I have! I've never wanted these dreams, remember? But this is the only way I can see to make it work! To make this world a better place!

KATIE

(*hands up*)

How is that going to work? Stone has to have his way. Period. Or it's the highway. He doesn't negotiate. He starts wars. He doesn't stop them until he is the victor. Just read his history. He. Will. *Never*. Stop.

Samuel folds his arms. His face softens.
Okay, you have my attention.

> SAMUEL

> So I'm supposed to just...just...*forget* about this?

> KATIE

> Yes!
>> (*pauses, sighs*)
> But I know how stubborn you are. You won't forget about it.
>> (*longer pause*)
> But if you do save this warmonger, don't expect a hero's welcome. And he will take the corridor.
>> (*shakes her head*)
> I can't talk about this anymore. Good night.

Katie storms out of the room. Samuel stares off after her, grabs his hat and puts it on.

His eyes say it all: I am trapped with no way out.

INT. LIVING ROOM – DAY

A light pierces the darkness of the early morning through the curtains. Samuel is dead to the world, his blankets wrapped in a jumbled mess around him.

As a large pillow hits his head, Samuel opens his eyes and groans in protest.

> KATIE
> (V.O.)
> Good morning birthday boy!

Katie grins, one hand behind her back. No reaction from Samuel.

> KATIE

Well, this is a first! Don't you like birthdays anymore?

                    SAMUEL
                   (*quietly*)
Not this time.

                    KATIE
                 (*arms folded*)
Okay, what's the matter, now? You pouting from last night's conversation?

Samuel sits up and runs his fingers through his hair. He barely shakes his head.

                    SAMUEL
I'm drafted.

                    KATIE
             (*angry breath intake*)
So that's why you're here? So you can hide?

                    SAMUEL
                  (*placating*)
And make the corridor. Don't worry. I'll be careful. If things don't work out, Father said I could make for Canada.

                    KATIE
                   (*snorts*)
Really? That old trick? Those days are long gone. Military police are stationed at the border, Samuel. They will hand deliver you to military prison. Guaranteed.

                    SAMUEL
                   (*panic*)

Then I need to stay with you. I'd be caught if I
lived at home.

KATIE
(*sighs*)
Well, all I can say is, keep a low profile! And
here...

Katie tosses him a package, shiny red wrapping.

KATIE
Happy 18th birthday, draft dodger!

Samuel rips it open to find a fancy black sketch pad.

KATIE
You know. For any more of your *ideas.*

SAMUEL
Thank you.

INT. PHYSICS CLASS – DAY

*Another advanced physics lecture ready to begin, with half a class attending.
Most students talk on their cell phones, looking like they want to be
somewhere else. The professor, very old school, writes a wave function
equation on a white board, with a erasable blue marker.*

*Jarrod enters and sees Samuel in his usual seat, midway down on the right,
by himself.*

JARROD
Samuel! Pssst! Samuel!

*Samuel turns and Jarrod urgently motions him to follow. Samuel leaps up
and joins him in the hall.*

INT. SMITH HALL -- DAY

SAMUEL
(*confused*)
Hi Jarrod. What's up?

JARROD
Sam! I mean, Samuel—sorry! Mr. Abraham and I
talked to Adara Jacinto last night!

A light dawns.

SAMUEL
The one who invested--

JARROD
(*snaps fingers*)
All that money for the wormhole project, yes!
She agreed to give us 12...million...dollars!

Samuel's eyes pop. Jarrod dances around the hall.

JARROD
And you know what else? President Hachmann
said we can use Research I Lab for *free*! You can
even quit auditing those classes! Isn't it great?

SAMUEL
(*serious*)
I like the classes.

JARROD
(*penitent*)
Oh right, fine, yes, keep going if you want. I was
just thinking that the project might take big
chunks of your time. But...but...can I be on your
team? It would be like a dream come true for me!
What do you say?

SAMUEL
(*considers*)
Yes. Of course.

Jarrod grins, grabs Samuel with both arms and shakes him playfully.

JARROD
Thanks a million, Samuel! This is so awesome! You are so totally awesome! Later!

Jarrod, on cloud nine, dances down the hall.

INT. PHYSICS CLASS -- DAY

Samuel catches Cameron before he leaves the lecture hall.

SAMUEL
Hey, Cameron. I wanted to ask about your dad.

Cameron stops short. Tenses.

CAMERON
Yeah, what about him?

SAMUEL
I was hoping you could give me some background information.

CAMERON
(*angry*)
Why? What did you hear?

SAMUEL
(*surprised*)
What?! Nothing. I just wanted to know more about his experience. Where he worked before.

CAMERON
(*relief*)
Oh.

(*pauses*)
He worked at the Glenn Research lab for eight
years. Then he was let go. Budget cuts, I think.
He never really talked about it. But he's really
smart and has a lot of connections. C'mon Sam,
you can trust him.

Samuel shrugs.

                    SAMUEL
        Okay. Thanks.

Samuel leaves.
Cameron stares at the floor, bug eyes revealing it all: I lied big time.

INT. RESEARCH I LAB -- DAY

Samuel wanders through aisle after aisle of sophisticated space equipment
and computers. Most is donated from NASA from years past.
A flash of light brings Samuel to the present.
Kyle holds a camera.

                    KYLE
        Historic day, Samuel! Truly historic!
                    (*pauses*)
        Pretty impressive, isn't it? All
        that equipment for our project. I
        mean, your project.

Samuel is lost in this huge new techno-world.

                    KYLE
        Ready for the meeting?

Kyle points to the meeting room.

INT. MEETING ROOM – DAY

Around a dark brown table sit Jarrod, Hillary, Cameron and two former NASA SCIENTISTS: Marc Prepp, early 60s with dark skin and balding head; and Emily Lerd, mid-60s, oriental features.

Samuel picks up his sketch pad and holds up a picture of his corridor within a simple door frame. Within the frame is a wooded landscape. Kyle snaps another picture.

> SAMUEL
>
> What I propose to build is a corridor that allows travel to anywhere on earth.

A beat.

> SAMUEL
>
> Kyle, I understand that in the past, you were able to control the location of where the wormholes emerged.

> KYLE
>
> *(nods proudly)*
>
> And we developed a protective dimensional shield that prevents the wormhole from collapsing. It opens wide enough to send objects out the other side.

> JARROD
>
> And you can control the direction of the hole for what ... a few hundred miles?

Kyle shakes his head and laughs.

> KYLE
>
> Up to 40,000 miles!

> MARC
>
> So...what exactly do you want to do with this device, Samuel?

Samuel clears his throat.

> SAMUEL
>
> Help people...save people.

MARC

So, only to promote peace?

SAMUEL

Yes.

EMILY

When you say, 'save people', what exactly does that mean?

SAMUEL

For instance if people were in danger, we could rescue them by walking through the portal, and pulling them back to safety. Back through the corridor. If they are starving, bring them food.

KYLE

Marc, I see no limits to this application. Wherever there is a need, we set it up and go. Taking a fraction of the time and manpower, it would save billions, or even trillions of dollars over time.

HILLARY

Imagine instant travel to your favorite getaway! Good-bye airlines, congestion and long commutes!

MARC

Samuel, I must admit I am duly impressed. This technology can help bring in a new era of transportation to our world. But how will you control its use? I mean, what if some day these are mass-produced and you no longer regulate how they are used? Can you see how they might be used for invasions, or kidnapping, or stealing priceless artifacts?

Samuel nods.

SAMUEL

We only need to make one.

Everyone looks perplexed. Cameron glances at Kyle then at Samuel.

CAMERON

Samuel...why only one? If we were careful we
could sell them for...millions...maybe much more,
and invest that money back into the project, or
whatever you wanted. And we could sell it only
to the right people—those who share our
interests. For the sake of peace.

SAMUEL

Because by only making one I control the way it
is used. How could you guarantee that those who
bought it wouldn't sell it to an enemy? Maybe in
the future we could make more, but for right
now, just one.

*Samuel glances over at Cameron. His eyes stay fixed on the table.
Kyle puts his hands in the air.*

KYLE

Okay Samuel, we'll do it your way. For now, we

make only one.

All team members nod in agreement.

INT. EXPERIMENTAL ROOM – DAY

*This room is filled with computers running complex programs, and open
spaces with holographic images showing wormhole reactions.
Samuel and Marc stand behind Emily, who navigates on her computer.*

EMILY

I'm using the NASA WORM project program,
but integrating smaller scale distance models.

MARC
Our biggest challenge will be the power cell
units, but I've got some ideas on how to work
with Samuel's formulas.

INT. GENERATOR ROOM—DAY

*Two large, thick glass windows look onto a huge AGC generator. Samuel,
Hillary and Emily set up tables and equipment.*

INT. POWER CELL CREATION ROOM – DAY

*A long wide table fills up the room. Hillary and Emily work side by side
carefully shaping red-black clay-type material into two steel brick-like
molds, aka power cells.*
*Two power cells, now fully cured, are carefully placed inside a metallic
briefcase, wired to the generator. Emily flips the power switch to
transfer energy to one cell. The briefcase glows yellow and dissolves
into thin air. Emily looks at Hillary and Samuel.*

EMILY
Back to square one.

INT. POWER CELL CREATION ROOM – ANOTHER DAY

*Emily and Hillary are at it again, trying to transfer power to a single
power cell: the briefcase holding the cell melts into a thick yellow gel.*

HILLARY
Back to square one?

Emily nods.

EXT. POWER CELL CREATION ROOM –
DAY

A power cell explodes, sending fragments of residue on the walls. Samuel, Jarrod and Cameron look at an exasperated Hillary.

Jarrod throws papers in the air and walks off.

Cameron looks bored.

SAMUEL

Maybe we should take a break?

Cameron shrugs.

INT. SMITH HALL LECTURE ROOM – DAY

We are halfway through an advanced physics lecture. This time Jarrod, Hillary and Cameron sit around Samuel, staring off into space.
The exit doors above abruptly open, and five SOLDIERS enter, armed with black discharge rifles. They march down the steps as the audience tenses.
One soldier talks to the professor in a low voice.
The professor and soldiers scan the room full of students.
Green scope lights dance around the room.

PROFESSOR

Samuel Miller? Is there a *Samuel Miller* here?

Samuel pales. We hear his racing heartbeat. He looks to his friends.

JARROD

Need some help?

Samuel looks at Jarrod. Then at the soldiers. He nods. Sweat builds on his brow.
Jarrod leaps up, runs out of the room and slams the door behind.
Soldiers rush up the stairs in pursuit. Samuel jumps up. Hillary grabs his arm.

HILLARY

(*whispers*)

No. Samuel. Stop! Don't panic.

Terror mode set in, Samuel flies out of the room.

> CAMERON
>
> Too late.

Cameron makes a call on his cell.

> CAMERON
> (*low voice*)
> Yeah, hey dad. Looks like we've got a problem.
> Sam's in trouble.

INT. HALLWAY – DAY

Samuel powers open the heavy double doors, knocking two SOLDIERS to the floor.

> SAMUEL
>
> Sorry!

Samuel tears out of the building. One soldier leaps to his feet, chases after.

> SOLDIER
>
> Hey, you! STOP!

The soldier blows a loud whistle.

EXT. SMITH HALL – DAY

Samuel sprints down the street.

He turns a corner and runs into several FEMALE STUDENTS, sending papers, texts, folders flying. Samuel falls headlong with them.

> SAMUEL
> (*breathless*)
> Sorry!

Samuel rolls back up, running into an...

EXT. ALLEY -- DAY

We see several tall, ivy covered buildings. A lone garbage can resides in the alley.

A brown cat leaps out of the can as Samuel sprints by.

More whistles shriek at high pitches and frequent intervals.

Samuel reaches the end of the alley and looks onto a busy street. Two military jeeps with SOLDIERS are parked on the far side.

Three jeeps scream past. Samuel ducks and turns around, his back against a wall. He slides down to a seated position, closes his eyes and covers his face.

> SAMUEL
> (*panic praying*)
> Help me. Please help me.

Car horns sound and Samuel opens his eyes. He watches more jeeps fly by.
Samuel pokes his head out and looks at traffic. Coast is clear. The Research I lab building is in sight.

Samuel blends with the crowds, weaving his way toward the lab. Another military jeep flies by. Samuel turns away just in time.
DOGS bark. Samuel turns to see two SOLDIERS with four Rottweilers closing in.

Samuel takes off. The soldiers let the dogs loose. They tackle Samuel to the ground and hold him with low growls. As a crowd gathers, one soldier pulls the dogs back. The other pulls Samuel to his feet and cuffs him.

> SOLDIER
> (*into radio*)
> Sir. We have the suspect in custody.

Kyle pulls up in a sporty red futuristic BMW. As it squeals to a stop, Kyle leaps out of the car and straight through the crowd.

KYLE
(*to the soldier*)
What's going on here?
(*to Samuel*)
Michael, are you all right? What happened?

SOLDIER
(*serious, surprised*)
Michael?

KYLE
(*agitated*)
Yes, my son, Michael. *Michael Smith.*

Kyle walks behind Samuel, pretends to pull a wallet out of his back pocket. He opens it and pulls out a piece of ID.

KYLE
Here. Michael Smith. Now what's this all about?

The soldiers look at each other, stymied.

SOLDIER
He ran, Mr. Smith. We thought he was Samuel Miller.

KYLE
(*peeved*)
And who is Samuel Miller? And why are you chasing him?

SOLDIER
He's a draft dodger.

> KYLE

Well, let me assure you gentlemen, no son of
mine is a draft dodger.

Kyle's face turns from deep frown to slight smile.
A military jeep drives up but the two soldiers motion them away.

> SOLDIER

I'm sorry Mr. Smith, but he ran. Michael, why
did you run away?

A beat.

Samuel stares at the ground as his cuffs are removed.

> KYLE
> (*to Samuel*)

Michael, why were you running?

> SAMUEL
> (*shrugs*)

They started chasing me.

> KYLE

All right. Let's go home.

Kyle guides Samuel and gently pushes him in the car. The soldiers
watch them carefully as Kyle drives away. They look at each other
and shrug.

INT. BMW – DAY

Kyle looks at Samuel, perplexed.

> KYLE

Why didn't you register as a student before your
draft? That's what we did with Cam.

> SAMUEL

(*stiffly*)

Where I come from, no one knew that was even possible. Why did you tell them I was Michael Smith? That was a lie.

Kyle looks at Samuel and laughs. Samuel sends daggers back.

KYLE

I saved your butt back there, Samuel Miller. Draft dodging lands you in jail, 45 days minimum. With an offense as serious as this, I thought you'd steer clear of it and really be the good kid you appear to be.

SAMUEL

I *am* good. I'm Amish. I hate war just like you.

(*hesitate*)

I just had to complete this project.
(*pause*)
Where did you get that fake ID?

KYLE

I know a trick or two, along with some smart connections who come in handy from time to time.
(*pause*)
But like you said, you need to finish the project, right? And I'm still on board with this to the end. And look, we gotta play smart from now on. This project is big, and it wouldn't be advisable to receive interference from the government. Right?

Samuel nods.

> KYLE

You might want to drop those classes you're auditing if you don't want any more of those military boys crashing our party. A lot safer that way.

Samuel sighs.

> SAMUEL

Thanks Kyle.

> KYLE

No problem. And don't worry about explaining this little episode. They just confused you with someone else.

Samuel looks unconvinced.

> SAMUEL

There's another Samuel Miller in Kent, Ohio?

Kyle shrugs and looks away.

INT. LAB OFFICE –NIGHT

Samuel sits at a medium-sized beige desk between stacks of papers. Engineering books lay open, and a laptop sits in front of him, running calculations and producing complex 3-D graphs.
His telephone rings. Samuel stares at it warily for a few seconds before answering.

> SAMUEL

Hello?

> KATIE
> (*filtered, strained*)

Hey.

> SAMUEL

Katie. What's wrong?

KATIE
(*filtered*)

Some soldiers came by. A few minutes ago. They think my brother Samuel is living with me.

SAMUEL
(*annoyed*)

Yeah, they thought I was him today. My *dad* came by just in time.

KATIE
(*filtered*)

Yeah, well Sergeant Haden and a few of his underlings don't seem to believe my story. I think they are still watching outside. Probably listening to our phone conversation.

SAMUEL

No doubt.

KATIE
(*filtered*)

So are you coming over?

SAMUEL

Maybe in a few days. All this lab work is piling up.

KATIE
(*filtered*)

All right, there's the nerd talking. And there's one more thing. I was fired today.

SAMUEL

What?!

KATIE
(*filtered*)

Something about a bad budget year. Though last month they talked about giving out bonuses. I couldn't get much out of them.

SAMUEL

What are you going to do?

KATIE
(*filtered*)

Find another job.

SAMUEL
(*excited*)

Join our team. I'll pay you five times what you were making before. See you tomorrow, okay?

KATIE
(*filtered laughs*)
And help you guys bring the world to an end?
(*pause*)
Let me think about it for a while. Bye.

Samuel hangs up and stares at his stacks of papers. He grabs one off the top and begins reading.

INT. POWER CELL CREATION ROOM – DAY

Emily and Hillary energize a pair of power cells inside yet another briefcase. The case retains its shape! They give each other a high five.

INT. LAB – DAY

Samuel, Cameron and Jarrod connect large Nikon Snapper 4307 lenses and Garmin Space Traveler 73 Rangefinders.

EXT. LAB PARKING LOT – DAY

Everyone helps load the equipment into two large white vans. Kyle and Cameron are driving.

KYLE

(*to Samuel*)

See you in a few days. They are broadcasting the launch on Thursday.

Kyle takes off. Cameron drives up beside Samuel and stops. He stares at the steering wheel.

He won't look at Samuel but it's obvious he has something to say.

He shakes his head as the van roars away.

KATIE (O.S.)

Samuel.

Samuel grins from ear to ear as he turns and hugs his sister.

SAMUEL

I was beginning to wonder if you were ever going to come!

KATIE

I have to play it cool with the feds hanging around, you know? But Samuel, that's what I wanted to talk to you about.

SAMUEL

What? What's wrong?

KATIE

This whole project!

(*pause*)

I can't —

SAMUEL

Can't? Can't what?

KATIE

Look, Samuel. Your dream is...well, *your* dream.
It never was mine. I mean it's great that you've
gotten this far and all, but....I can't work for you.

SAMUEL

Because?

KATIE

Because of *him*. I see no logical reason in saving a
man who would kill millions just to meet his oil
quotas.

SAMUEL
(*Sotto voce*)

Okay.

KATIE

But if you need anything from me...like me to go
with you somewhere, or get something, I'll do it.
(*pause*)
Not for him. Never for him. But always for you.
Okay?

SAMUEL

Thanks Katie. So what are you going to do?

KATIE

(*forced smile*)
I'll find my place. Don't worry about me.

JARROD
(O.S.)

Hey Samuel. Could you come over here for a minute?

Katie begins to walk away but Samuel stops her with a raised hand.
He pulls out a wad of bills and puts it in her hand.
Katie looks at Samuel, suspicious.

> KATIE
> You know I can't accept this...blood money.

> SAMUEL
> (*smiles*)
> Birthday money from Father. I haven't spent any since
> I've been with you. Consider it a rent contribution.

> KATIE
> (*relieved*)
> In that case, duly accepted!

INT. RESEARCH LAB MEETING ROOM – DAY

Samuel, Jarrod and Hillary watch the large screen TV and scarf popcorn
as a rocket launches their payload into space. Jarrod whoops it up.

> SAMUEL
> So...the six satellites we are sending up...how much did
> they cost?

> HILLARY
> About $60 million dollars.

Samuel's mouth flies open.

> SAMUEL
> But we have only $12 million!

> HILLARY
> (*shrugs*)
> Kyle arranged special financing with a company
> called Satellite Systems.

> JARROD

Hey, don't worry! Sooner or later more people
will invest in this project...once they understand
what it can do.

Samuel's eyes are big as saucers.
A news anchor appears on screen.

ANCHOR MAN

In other news, President Stone has confirmed his
next appearance in the Middle East will take
place next month in Iran--

Jarrod flips off the TV.

JARROD
(*pinches mouth*)

Who cares?

INT. LAB – DAY

The frame of a doorway stands propped between two power cells, fully
charged, out of their "briefcases". Five feet beyond this is a second pair of
power cells, laying parallel with the first two. Looking from above, they
form a rectangle. The door frame is cordoned off with tape marked in big
*bold letters: **"CAUTION"**.*

Samuel types on his laptop. The image of his father's house comes up inside
the door frame.

JARROD
Samuel! You did it! Look at that!!

Emily shakes her head.

EMILY
Only a picture from our satellite feed. Watch this.

Emily tosses a small rubber ball at the corridor. It ricochets back violently
and puts a hole in the wall behind them.

EMILY

We have to fine tune the corridor and power cells so they can calibrate the same distances.

JARROD

Once this is fine-tuned, how long will the corridor stay open?

EMILY

Three minutes.

JARROD

That's it?

EMILY

The cells can only control the power flow for a short period. We go beyond that time and they always explode.

Samuel stands in front of the corridor. Cameron types on a laptop. He shakes his head.

CAMERON
(*to Samuel*)

All right, try it now.

Samuel rolls a ball but it ricochets, at Cameron who ducks just in time. Samuel fetches the ball, Cameron types more into the computer and gives a thumbs up. Samuel rolls the ball, it bounces back and takes out a window.

CAMERON

I don't get it. Why won't this work? We went over the equations a million times! Something else must be wrong.

SAMUEL

Try the rotational simulator control. Equilibrate it to the value of minus one.

CAMERON

I tried that yesterday, at minus two.

SAMUEL

Try minus one. Please.

CAMERON

(*sighs*)

I'm going out of my mind.

Cameron types in the command.

CAMERON

All right, one more time.

Samuel rolls the ball and again it snaps back, breaking some lights in the process.
Cameron pounds on the desk, throws some papers in the air and leaves.

EXT. KATIE'S HOUSE -- NIGHT

It's blustery and raining buckets.
Samuel pounds on the door and Katie swings it open.

SAMUEL

Is the coast clear?

KATIE

Funny, *Michael.* What's up?

SAMUEL

I'm hungry and miss your cooking!

KATIE

Get in here, you draft dodger.

INT. KATIE'S HOUSE – NIGHT

Samuel relaxes on the couch, channel surfing until he finds a news station. Katie sits at the kitchen table, sifting through her mail.

KATIE
(O.S)

Bills...junk mail...hey, a real letter.

ANCHOR WOMAN

Today the President ordered twenty thousand more troops to the Middle East, this time to Egypt, Libya and Jordan.

We see PRESIDENT STONE, stout and grey-haired, parading before a news audience. His face is hard, his eyes piercing.

PRESIDENT STONE

Recent developments in the Middle East leave me no choice but to station my forces in and around those countries deemed to be ripe for terrorist attacks. Oil supplies around the world continue to be targets of increasingly hostile enemies, bent on bringing chaos to our world. Rest assured I will not let this happen. Today we welcome Nigeria's President Zwary and Prime Minister Lofti to our coalition.

ANCHOR WOMAN

In related news, reports of President Stone sightings are on the rise, apparently the result of counterfeits attempting to gain access into sensitive government facilities—

KATIE (O.S.)

(*strained*)

Samuel!

Samuel flips off the TV. Joins her at the table.

SAMUEL

Yes?

Katie hands him a letter. She begins to cry.

SAMUEL

From Father!
(*eyes wary*)
My dear children. I am writing you with sad
news. Your grandmother Priscilla went to be
with the Lord last Monday. Today we laid her
body to rest. I am sorry I did not contact you
before. With the recent storms, the telephone did
not work and I could not ride into the city.
(*swallows*)
Please pass this news to your brother. With love,
Father.

KATIE
(*sniffs*)
I would have gone to her funeral.

SAMUEL
Me too.

Samuel reads the letter again, but to himself.

SAMUEL
What about Amos? We have to tell him.

KATIE
(*shrugs*)
I don't know where he is.

SAMUEL

You haven't seen him in seven years?

KATIE

He sends birthday and Christmas cards, and
always signs it "Commander Amos". There's
never a return address. I wouldn't know where to
look for him.

SAMUEL

You should go back home to visit. They would
like to see you.

Katie crosses her arms and glares at the floor.

SAMUEL

You know I'm right.

KATIE

No, Samuel, I don't know you're right. Did
Father *ask* me to visit? Did he *say* he needed me?

*Samuel slowly shakes his head as a light begins to
dawn.*

KATIE

When I left, I left for good. I am
never...going...back.
(*pause*)
I can take you to the bus station tomorrow.

SAMUEL

I can't. Too much work to finish.

KATIE

You know what you need? You need to get out
of this town. Come to church with me
tomorrow.

SAMUEL
(*mouth slackens*)

You go to church?

KATIE

Yes, I go to church, Samuel. Every Sunday.
And where are you on Sundays?

SAMUEL
(*quiet, red-faced*)

At the lab.
(*hesitates*)

Where do you go?

KATIE

The Mennonite church in Aurora. A drive will
do you some good. And so will going to church.

SAMUEL
(*sulk*)

It's not the same as back home.

KATIE
(*deep sigh*)

Of course not. It never will be.

*Katie storms out of the kitchen to her room. We hear the door
slam.*
*Samuel slumps on the couch, holding his hat. He turns it this way
and that. Tears form in his eyes.*

EXT. MENNONITE CHURCH -- MORNING

Rain mixes with mostly snow in a strong wind.

A small grey church building connects to a half-filled, weathered parking lot. Katie parks her Mazda close to the entrance. Samuel and Katie hurry inside.

INT. CHURCH – MORNING

The congregation bows for silent prayer.
Samuel closes his eyes and prays for a moment.
He opens his eyes and they widen.

EXT. CHURCH PARKING LOT – LATE MORNING

Samuel grins as he takes Katie's hand and playfully pulls her toward the car.

> KATIE
> (*surprised*)
> So what's up with you? You've been twitching since our prayers.

> SAMUEL
> (*very excited*)
> I know what we need! I know how to fix it! The power cells are wrongly programmed because—

Katie laughs and holds up her hand.

> KATIE
> All right, Mr. Scientist. I see that my church has done you some good after all. I'll take you back to your precious lab.

> SAMUEL
> (*grins*)
> Thanks Katie!

INT. LAB – DAY

Our focus is on the door frame of the corridor. Emily finishes typing and gives Samuel the nod. Kyle stands in the background with two GUESTS, a well-dressed middle aged man and woman.

An image of a field appears in the doorway, with Marc standing in it. Samuel grabs a ball. Sweat runs along his forehead.

> JARROD
> (*twitching*)

Do it Samuel!

> CAMERON
> (*leaning forward*)

Go for it Samuel!

> SAMUEL
> (*swallows*)

Here we go.

Samuel rolls the ball toward the doorway. It travels over the threshold and instantly reappears in the park on the other side. Marc picks up the ball and waves it in the air.

> JARROD

Awesome! Awesome! Awesome! We did it!

> KYLE

Congratulations Samuel!

Jarrod grabs a ball twice the size of the last one.

> JARROD

My turn. Ready?

Samuel gives him the nod and Jarrod rolls the ball. It disappears and reappears in the park. Another success.

Kyle walks up to Samuel with his two guests.

> KYLE
> (*all smiles*)
> Samuel, this is Barton Gage and Abigael
> Crawford. After listening to my spiel and
> watching your performance just now, they agreed
> to invest $5 million into our project.

> SAMUEL
> (*excited*)
> Thank you. Thank you very much!

Everyone starts clapping and shouting, led by Jarrod, who leads a dance around the room.

INT. KATIE'S DINING ROOM -- NIGHT

Samuel and Katie eat a celebration dinner: steak, potatoes and salad.

> KATIE
>
> I'm proud of you Samuel. I mean it. I really am.

> SAMUEL
> (*clutches hands*)
> Tomorrow we test it with animals.
> If that works, we test it on people.

> KATIE
>
> Already?

Samuel nods vigorously.

KATIE
I'm glad that's not me! Who are
you going to——

*Samuel is grinning from ear to ear. Katie drops
her fork.*

KATIE
You?

A strong nod.

KATIE
(*worried*)
And if something goes wrong?

SAMUEL
Nothing bad will happen.
(*pause*)
And I want you to meet me...at Father's house.

Katie stares at Samuel, expressionless.

SAMUEL
Please?

KATIE
On the road. Near the house. That's it.

SAMUEL
Fair enough. And don't worry. It'll work.
KATIE
And after you save the President? What will you
do?

SAMUEL
(*shrugs*)
Go back home, I suppose.

KATIE

Aren't you forgetting about the
draft? Your draft!

SAMUEL

I'm saving his life, remember? He should at least
overlook my draft. But anyway.
(*clears throat*)
My work will be done.

KATIE

Done? You can't be serious! Remember all those
things you said could be done with it? Rescue
people in floods? Bring food to starving people?
Why stop with one bloodthirsty dictator?

SAMUEL
(*offended*)

Maybe I should give it to you and let you make
all the decisions.

A beat.
Katie folds her arms.

KATIE

Maybe you should.

Samuel throws her a blazing look.

INT. KATIE'S HOUSE -- DAY

*Samuel reads an advanced physics book while Katie watches the
news.*

ANCHOR MAN

...in light of the continuing need for American
military servicemen, we bring you a story about
some communities that have been torn apart by
the draft. Terry Robinson explains more.

TERRY ROBINSON, reporter in her thirties, with long, dark hair, stands on a dirt road with a rural backdrop.

TERRY

Those who dwell in these communities are known as the Amish, a people who have strong moral objections to any type of aggression, especially war. Yet the Amish communities have been hit especially hard since most of their young men have been drafted. Of those able to return from military service, more than 70 percent are unable to adjust back to this simple lifestyle, and choose instead to find their own place in our world. For News Channel Seven, I'm Terry Robinson.

Katie turns off the TV.

KATIE

Can you believe it? Seventy percent don't come back!

SAMUEL

Daniel was drafted.

KATIE
(wide eyes)

When?

SAMUEL

Two days before I left home. He asked about you.

KATIE
(amused)

Daniel Beiler. He used to say he wanted to marry me!

SAMUEL

He still does.

INT. LAB – DAY

*The corridor is powered up. A farm field appears in the doorway,
with Samuel, Cameron, Hillary, Jarrod and Emily gathered
around. Cameron holds a beagle in his arms.*

Kyle stands in the background, talking on his cell.

*Samuel teases the dog with a raw steak, then tosses it into the corridor.
Cameron releases the dog and it bounds into the corridor with a happy bark
and disappears. It instantly reappears in the farm field, gulping down the
meat.*

*Hillary opens a wire cage next to the doorway. Monarch butterflies pass
through the corridor, and fly off into the sky.*

Emily coaxes a rabbit to pass through the corridor.

*Jarrod pushes, cajoles, and threatens a small horse until it sees the
pasture of grass and walks through.*

EXT. FARM -- DAY

Marc scurries back and forth trying to catch all the animals. They run

off, apparently enjoying the freedom.

INT. LAB – DAY

*Cameron and Hillary kiss. Jarrod and Emily laugh. Kyle shakes
Samuel's hand and Jarrod leads a dance around the room.*

INT. LAB—DAY

*Cameron, Jarrod, Hillary, Emily and Marc line up in front of the corridor.
ADARA JACINTO, 50's, prim and proper, stands beside Samuel,
watching him type on his laptop. Kyle stands in the background,
talking on his cell. An image of a road and farm field appears in the
corridor-it's an early spring day. Katie stands by the road, leaning
against her Miata.*

EVERYONE

Good luck, Samuel.

Samuel puts on his hat. He shakes hands with everyone as they line up. He walks toward the corridor. Hesitates for only a few seconds. In slow motion we see Samuel pass through the doorway. He disappears and then reappears on the road next to Katie. Samuel grins, tips his hat and bows.

EXT. ROAD -- DAY

Katie grabs Samuel and hugs him. They laugh.

They turn to see a horse and buggy, stopped about 20 feet away, carrying an Amish man and his wife. Samuel and Katie wave. The Amish couple, with eyes wide, return the wave before turning the buggy around.

> SAMUEL
> That will start some tongues wagging.

> KATIE
> (*laughs*)
> For at least twenty years. Let's go!

> SAMUEL
> Please wait. There's something else I need your help with.

> KATIE
> Yeah?

> SAMUEL
> This is really important. Remember you promised to help me...to go with me?

> KATIE
> And?

> SAMUEL
> I need you to go with me...

> KATIE
> (*pause*)

To help you save *him*? Why can't you ask your friends?

> SAMUEL

They won't understand why. They speak of him like he's the devil incarnate. So no, Katie. You are the only one who knows.

Katie turns around, shakes her fists and sighs deeply.

> KATIE
> (Sotto voce)

Why me?

She turns back around.

> KATIE

Okay...where?

> SAMUEL

Iran.

INT. MEETING ROOM -- DAY

A lunch celebration is underway, main course: tacos. Several bottle of champagne are open, along with cakes, cookies and ice cream.

> KYLE
> (*to Emily and Marc*)

I can't thank both of you enough for your help on this project. I hope your bonus money made it worthwhile!

Emily and Marc look embarrassed, but they nod.

> MARC

Very rewarding project.

> KYLE

What's next for you guys?

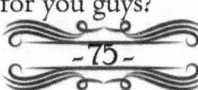

EMILY

We've been contracted with Canaveral for a pilot program. A new space project. We fly out at three.

CAMERON

I can't wait! After this semester I'm going to Hawaii! How about it, dad?

KYLE

You know me, Cam. Austin Lake.

CAMERON

Yeah. I know. The cabin.
(*to Hillary*)
He loves Montana!

HILLARY

I'm thinking Hawaii! A free trip!

Samuel eats his taco in the background. Adara walks over to him.

ADARA

So Samuel, what's next for your corridor?

SAMUEL

(*quietly, to Adara*)
I have to go away for a while. And I need your help.

ADARA

(*pause*)
All right. What can I do?

INT. KATIE'S HOUSE – NIGHT

Samuel mumbles in his sleep, tossing and turning. We hear sounds coming from his dream: of jets, helicopters, machine gun fire, and screaming. Samuel jerks up and holds his head.

SAMUEL

Katie!

The hall light comes on and Katie appears.

SAMUEL
(*quietly*)
It's time.

EXT. UNIVERSITY AIRPORT HANGAR -- DAY

Large and small planes are parked next to their prospective hangars. A light rain falls from the gray morning sky. Samuel and Katie stand beside Adara, who motions to her private jet.

ADARA

It's fully automatic. The onboard computer will respond to your voice commands.

SAMUEL
(*eye twitches*)
No pilot?

ADARA
(*smiles*)

Not to worry, Samuel.

KATIE

Any advice about Tehran?

ADARA

Our military controls just about everything there. I've arranged for you to be escorted out of the airport. From there you can take a taxi or bus.
(*pause*)
Samuel, I wanted to ask you about Kyle.
(*hesitates*)

Did you tell him what you are doing?

SAMUEL

No. Why?

KATIE

Maybe he caught wind of your harebrained
scheme and wants to stop it.

Adara laughs.

ADARA

Maybe.

Adara holds out her hand and he takes it at once.

ADARA

This is a very noble act on your part, Samuel. But
be careful. And good luck.

*Samuel releases her hand. Adara waves and walks
off. Samuel stares at the plane.*

SAMUEL

I don't know, Katie. No
pilot?

KATIE

Your call, little brother. But you know they'll
screen you on a commercial flight.

*Samuel gives a determined stare, climbs up the steps and slowly walks
inside. Katie follows.*

INT. JET -- DAY

*The cockpit computer console is lit up with a hundreds of buttons, switches
and lights.*

Samuel and Katie hurriedly buckle as the computer initiates the engine startup procedure.

> COMPUTER
>
> Good morning. Please prepare for immediate departure.

Samuel looks at Katie and they laugh.

EXT. OVER THE ATLANTIC – DAY

The jet screams through the air. Huge dark storm clouds loom.
Lightning flashes all around.
Samuel sits white knuckled in his seat as the plane rattles.

INT. JET -- DAY

Lightning flashes through the windows.
Samuel closes his eyes.

> SAMUEL
>
> This was a mistake.

> KATIE
>
> Great. Now you tell me. Why didn't you change your mind before we left the airport?

Samuel shakes his head. The jet really vibrates.

> SAMUEL
>
> Taking the plane is the mistake. I sh-sh-sh-should have f-f-figured out another way...

EXT. JET -- DAY

A bolt of lightning cuts through the sky next to the plane.

EXT. MEHRABAD AIRPORT – DAY

The jet lands and parks. A military escort waits for Samuel and Katie.

EXT. MOTAHRI MOSQUE, TEHRAN, IRAN -- DAY

President Stone struts behind a podium, addressing a crowd of reporters and Iranian officials, sitting on folding chairs. By his side stands Secretary of Defense ROBERT SKILLER and dozens of Secret Service BODYGUARDS surround the scene.

PRESIDENT STONE

...many would doubt my purpose and the intentions of this distinguished administration. But I have come in good faith...

INT. MOTAHRI MOSQUE, FRONT ROOM -- DAY

Samuel looks out the window. Katie stands by his side.

SAMUEL

Are you ready?

Katie, now looking pale, nods.

INT. PRAYER HALL – DAY

A few ancient and beautiful vases and sculptures decorate the room. Samuel and Katie walk to a wooden platform, beneath which Katie hides. Samuel hands her his laptop, then secures the platform. He kneels down by the floor.

SAMUEL
Good luck!

KATIE
(O.S.)

Be careful!

Samuel runs out of the room.

EXT. MOSQUE – DAY

> PRESIDENT STONE
> ...we have no choice but to preserve that which
> will help us all to survive...

*Military helicopters ROAR in the background. The President looks
agitated and pauses. He returns to his speech.*

> PRESIDENT STONE
> We will bring more soldiers to the aid of our
> friends until this crisis ends, and our foes no
> longer pose a threat...

*Two military jets swoop around the mosque's minarets and close in,
attack-style. Live cameras turn to the jets as they spray the crowd with a
hail of bullets.*

> PRESIDENT STONE
> WHAT THE?

*The President is knocked down and covered by his bodyguards.
Several in the crowd are hit, including the Secretary of Defense.
The crowd scatters. Secret Servicemen return FIRE with their guns.
Three military helicopters land. Marines pour out and FIRE on the
fleeing bystanders.*

*Four SECRET SERVICEMEN pull the President to his feet and run to
the mosque. One is shot and falls to the ground.*

INT. MOSQUE ENTRANCE -- DAY

*Samuel backs away from the window, his eyes wide. He turns and runs out
of the room.
The front door is kicked open. The President and two of his
BODYGUARDS, Karlik and Snipes, run in. Another trailing bodyguard,
wounded, signals for them to leave. He guards the door.
The President and his two men run down the hall.*

INT. PRAYER HALL – DAY

Samuel stands near the corridor. The image is only darkness. The President's bodyguards enter and begin a search for cover.

PRESIDENT STONE

(*shouting*)

What is going on? Who ordered this attack?
Those morons...they are my soldiers!!! They work
for me! They don't shoot me!

SAMUEL

Mr. President!

Snipes turns and fixes his gun on Samuel.

PRESIDENT STONE

What do you want?

SAMUEL

I want to save your life, Mr. President. I can
show you the way to safety.

Machine gun fire erupts in the hall. The President slowly walks toward Samuel.

PRESIDENT STONE

You want to save *me*? Save me from them? From
out there?

Samuel points to the corridor in earnest.

SAMUEL

(*pleading*)

Please, Mr. President. This is your only way of
escape. You must go now! Just walk through
here. It will take you back to your office in
Washington.

Karlik peers into the corridor.
Snipes keeps his gun trained on Samuel.

The President shoves Karlik aside and looks into the corridor.
He stares at Samuel.

> PRESIDENT STONE
> (*angry*)
> So that's what this is all about? So I'll change my
> mind and buy your corridor? You dirty--

> SAMUEL
> What? No, Mr. President, I will never sell it.

> PRESIDENT STONE
> That's not what I heard. I was quoted a billion
> dollars. *Each.*

Eight soldiers rush into the room, guns drawn.

> SOLDIER
> Get 'em!

In slow motion the soldiers open fire. The president takes a shot to his right
shoulder.

Karlik returns fire, hitting a soldier in the chest, then ducks and runs, grabs
the President and disappears into the corridor.

Snipes, using Samuel as a shield, shoots a soldier in the head. The
soldier falls.

Soldiers fire back. Samuel is shot in the stomach and he collapses.

His face contorts as he is dragged into the corridor and
disappears. The corridor vanishes.

INT. OVAL OFFICE, WHITE HOUSE -- NIGHT

Karlik leads the halting President to a couch.
Samuel is curled up on the floor, unconscious and bleeding
heavily.

PRESIDENT STONE

(*shouts*)

Tell those soldiers to stand
down!
(*looks at Samuel*)
How pathetic. It's just a kid.

*The President paces, twitching and shaking. He grabs books from his
shelves and throws them around the room.*
*He grabs the desk phone and hurls it, breaking against the wall. Papers and
books follow.*

PRESIDENT STONE

Service!

Several SECRET SERVICEMEN enter.

PRESIDENT STONE

Get him off my floor and clean up his mess.
(*to Snipes*)
Get him to surgery. Use Casi to find out what he
knows.

Snipes turns to leave.

PRESIDENT STONE

And Snipes.

SNIPES

Yes, Mr. President?

PRESIDENT STONE

I want that corridor.

SNIPES

Yes, Mr. President.

*Snipes and two others carry Samuel out of the room. Karlik and four
other servicemen attend to the President.*

INT. BETHESDA MEDICAL CENTER, OPERATING ROOM -- NIGHT

Several masked SURGEONS and NURSES hover over Samuel. The heart monitor reveals it all: he is slipping away. Snipes stands off to one side, looking bored and reading on his tablet.

> SURGEON I
> (*to nurse*)
> Another blood transfusion!

The nurse hurries out of the room.

> SURGEON 2
> Hold on young fella. Just hold on.

The surgeon moves his instruments deep inside Samuel's body, and retrieves a bullet. He drops it on a tray.

> SURGEON 2
> Nice one!

Samuel goes flatline.

> SURGEON I
> We're losing him!

The surgeons start shouting orders at the nurses. Their voices fade to echoes of noise. We enter Samuel's mind into —

EXT. FIELD – DAY

GRANDFATHER ISAAC, GRANDMOTHER PRISCILLA and Samuel, all young children, laugh and run through green lush fields of wheat. Isaac wears a smaller version of the hat Samuel was given. He suddenly stops, turns around and looks at Samuel.

ISAAC

Samuel? Why are you here?

Samuel looks confused, but can only shrug.

PRISCILLA
(*urgent*)
Go back home, Samuel! Go back home!

Isaac hands Samuel his hat as Priscilla shoos him away. Samuel reaches out to touch her but she disappears.

SAMUEL
(*loud*)

Grandma!

We return to —

INT. OPERATING ROOM – NIGHT

Samuel's vitals slowly stabilize. The surgeons stare at him then at each

other.

SURGEON 1

I was sure we lost him.

SURGEON 2

Good thing he came back. It would have been our jobs.

SURGEON 1
(*shakes his head*)

It would have been a lot worse than that. All right people, let's clean up.

INT. ICU RECOVERY ROOM – DAY

Samuel lies in bed, unconscious, with tubes and wires attached. Snipes sits nearby reading some news on his tablet, looking bored.

The door flies open, and in parades CASI STONE, 20, and in charge. Female BODYGUARDS, Tamarah and Nari, armed to the teeth, accompany her. Both wear dark sunglasses and have one look: don't mess with me. Casi eyes Snipes.

> CASI
>
> Who let you out of your kennel?

> SNIPES
>
> Well. Look who has graced us with a visit.

> CASI
>
> You were supposed to tell me about him. But you can leave now.

Snipes stands and looks her in the eye.

> SNIPES
>
> Nothing ever changes with you, does it, Ms. Stone?

Casi draws her 9mm on him. Nari and Tamarah do the same.

> CASI
>
> My finger feels sort of twitchy.

> SNIPES
>
> Aren't you tired of playing games, Ms. Stone?

Snipes grins as he leisurely walks out. Nari follows him. Casi studies Samuel's face. A look passes over her.

> CASI

(*annoyed*)

Of course. It figures.

Casi attaches a tiny transmitter to the back of Samuel's head. She looks at Tamarah, who stares back.

CASI

What?

Tamarah looks away.

INT. ROOM 214 – DAY

Samuel's eyes slowly open to see everything in his room: TV, monitoring machines, small windows. Casi, Nari and Tamarah on his right.

CASI

Hello Samuel.

Samuel looks at Casi blankly.

CASI

I'm Casi Stone. I'm here to get some answers.

SAMUEL
(*gravelly voice*)

About what?

CASI
(*laughs*)

About what? Now, that's good.

Samuel looks at his tubes and wires.

SAMUEL

I need to go home. Now.

CASI

Home? Hmmmm. I don't think so.

Samuel shakes his head.

SAMUEL

I've had enough. I'm done. I'm going home.

Samuel pulls the tubes and wires from his body, forces himself up.

He sways.

Casi stares at Samuel and smirks.

Samuel returns her look.

SAMUEL

Go ahead...laugh.

Casi stands aside as Samuel struggles to reach the door. He swoons and falls. He gets up and falls again. Gets up.

Once more and he reaches the door knob.

He looks inside his gown to see blood rapidly soaking through the bandage over his stomach.
He opens the door to find two SOLDIERS standing in front of him.
Samuel collapses and they haul him back to bed.

SAMUEL
(angry)

Let me go home!

A mist forms in his eyes. Casi gently touches Samuel's hand. He pulls it away. Casi pulls her hand back.

A NURSE enters and reconnects Samuel's tubes and wires.
Samuel closes his eyes.

CASI
(quietly to herself)
It was only a dream. It didn't mean anything.

SAMUEL
(*short*)

But that's why I'm here.

INT. ROOM 214 – TWO DAYS LATER

Samuel watches the news. His ankle is cuffed to his bed.

ANCHOR WOMAN

We continue our coverage of 'America in Crisis'. Two weeks after the President was shot, 20 American generals have disappeared from as many countries around the world. Fifteen U.S. embassies have been bombed, and President Stone has yet to come out of his seclusion. Although no one has publicly declared responsibility for these recent events, rumors abound that the group calling itself 'The Freedom Force' may be involved.
(*pauses*)

In other news, last night Mexico City was hit with the worst earthquake in recent history, as thousands are believed dead –

Casi enters the room. Samuel flips off the TV.

CASI

Catching up on the news?

SAMUEL
(*glares*)

And?

CASI
(*shrugs*)

Don't know. Thought you might have a conscience.

SAMUEL

(*annoyed*)

A conscience. What are you talking about? I
saved your father!

CASI

Don't give me that hero crap. He's gone into
hiding because of you. You'll probably get the
death penalty.

SAMUEL

(*really annoyed*)

WHAT?

CASI

Well, what did you think? That you could
blackmail the President of the United States into
buying your invention? That you could plan his
assassination? And at the same time sell it to his
enemies!

*Samuel jerks up in bed, heedless of the blood soaking through his
shirt again.*

SAMUEL

(*testy*)

WHAT? You're crazy! It's not for sale. I would
never sell it to anyone. Ever!

CASI

How else are they getting into the embassies,
Samuel? How else could these generals disappear?

Samuel stares at her, oblivious.

CASI

You are in serious trouble.

Samuel looks away.

SAMUEL

(*to himself*)

I should have listened to Katie. This is all wrong. This wasn't supposed to happen!

CASI

Well, it did and you messed up big time.

SAMUEL

I don't believe you. I can't believe you. Please leave.

CASI

You might have saved my father, but your invention is about to destroy our world.

Casi leaves.
Samuel's eyes are big as saucers.

INT. ROOM 214 -- NIGHT

Samuel sits up in his bed, head in hands. His eyes are red. Casi enters, totally in control.

CASI

So you're not eating? Is this a hunger strike?

Samuel glares at her.

CASI

I wish I could help you. I really do. But I can't interfere.

SAMUEL

(*sad, haunted eyes*)

I won't help you. I will never sell or give the corridor to anyone. Ever.

Casi's eyes bore into him.

CASI

We're beyond that argument.

SAMUEL

All my life I dreamed of saving your father by
creating this corridor. All I wanted to do was
obey the dream and then go back home. That's
all.

Samuel looks at Casi with convincing eyes.
You have to believe me.
Casi stares at him for a minute. A look comes over her and she turns away.

CASI

Your father is worried about you.
And your mother...she misses you.

Samuel stares at Casi as she walks out. He closes his eyes and shakes
his head. Samuel flips on the TV.

REPORTER

With President Stone still in hiding and news of
more U.S. embassies under attack across the
world, it is now unclear how long this nation will
remain under Marshall Law—

Samuel flips off the TV and flings the remote. It hits the screen and
breaks into pieces.

INT. ROOM 214 -- NIGHT

The lights come on. Casi enters, flanked by Tamarah and Nari who pushes
a man in a wheelchair. But his face somehow looks exactly like Samuel's.
Tamarah closes the door. Casi touches Samuel's hand and he wakes.

CASI

Time to go, Samuel.
(*points to wheelchair*)
Here's your replacement.

SAMUEL

What? Now you believe me?

CASI

Not you. Your mother.

Samuel looks at the slumped corpse in the wheelchair in alarm.
SAMUEL

What's going on?

Nari unlocks and removes Samuel's cuffs while Tamarah pulls out the wires and tubes. Samuel shrinks back.

CASI

We're here to get you out. Your only chance is to come with us.

SAMUEL

You killed that man and now you say I should I trust you? How do I know you won't kill me?

CASI

Samuel, this was Karlik. Remember Karlik? Snipes' partner? He's wearing a mask.

SAMUEL

You *killed* him?

CASI

We only have a few minutes before the video feed comes online and the guards return. If that happens you will never escape! Is that what you want?

An intense alarm sounds. Samuel covers his ears.

SAMUEL

(*to Casi*)

Now what did you do?

CASI

Nothing! Alarms go off here all the time!

Samuel looks at Casi wryly.
The alarm stops.
Tamarah pulls Samuel out of bed.

SAMUEL

My clothes! Wait! I need my clothes!
Samuel's clothes hit him. Nari smirks.

CASI

Samuel, hurry and change!

SAMUEL

(*folds his arms*)

In front of you? No way!

Casi is caught off guard by his refusal.

CASI

(*shouts*)

Then get in the bathroom!

SAMUEL

You don't need to yell at me, Casi Stone. I can
hear you just fine!

Samuel slowly makes his way to the bathroom, while holding his stomach.
He closes and locks the door.

CASI

(*groans*)

I don't believe this!

NARI

(*cocks her gun*)

I can make him hurry up.

Casi shakes her head.

CASI

Just get Karlik ready.

Nari and Tamarah lift Karlik's body off the wheelchair and set it in the bed. They cuff the foot, place the body sideways and cover it with a blanket. We hear talking and footsteps in the hallway. Casi, Nari and Tamarah dive under the bed.

A MILITARY POLICE OFFICER and NURSE enter.

NURSE

I heard noises.

The nurse looks at the body.

NURSE

He's sleeping.
> (*pause*)

Wait.

MP

What?

A beat.

NURSE

What's this wheelchair doing here?

The MP walks slowly around the room, gun in hand. He stands over Karlik's body.

Casi and her bodyguards are poised under the bed, guns readied.

NURSE
> (*insisting*)

We need to let him sleep. Let's go.

The nurse takes the wheelchair and they leave.

Samuel slowly opens the bathroom door and looks out. Casi, Nari and Tamarah emerge.

> CASI
> (*gritted teeth*)

Are you ready yet?

> SAMUEL

What happened to my wheelchair?

> CASI

You get to walk.

INT. HALLWAY – NIGHT

Samuel slowly walks beside Casi. He grimaces and Casi takes his arm.

> CASI

Here, let me help-

Samuel pulls away.

> SAMUEL

No, thank you.

Tamarah pushes the elevator button. Nari acts as lookout.

> GUARD (V.O.)
> Hey!

A GUARD runs toward them.
Nari pulls out a gas grenade.

> SAMUEL
> (*to Nari*)

Stop!

Casi motions and Nari pockets the grenade.

> GUARD

(all grins)
Casi Stone? Casi Stone! I thought it was you! I
was with you and your father last year in Costa
Rica. You probably don't even remember me!

Casi shakes his outstretched hand.

CASI
No, I don't but thanks!

NARI
Miss Stone...he's bleeding through again.

CASI
Wish we could stay and talk but we have to get
him to surgery. Stiches came out again.

The guard stares at the blood on Samuel's shirt.
He shrugs his shoulders and walks away.
The elevator opens.

INT. ELEVATOR -- NIGHT

Samuel leans against the wall. He closes his eyes and coughs. His face pales.

SAMUEL

Where are you taking me?

Nari and Tamarah look away.

SAMUEL
Will they find me? Your father, I mean.

CASI
It's not my father who's coming after you Samuel.

SAMUEL

Then...who...

The elevator door opens. Agent Snipes stands in front of them, smiling. His gun is drawn.

CASI
(*to Samuel*)

You had to ask?

SNIPES

Hello Casi. Have you seen Karlik?
(*cocks his gun*)
Hello, Samuel.

Snipes points his gun at Samuel and grins.
Nari mashes the elevator button.
Casi leaps out and karate kicks Snipes in the stomach. Snipes falls back to the floor.
Tamarah pulls Casi into the elevator. The door slams shut.

INT. HOSPITAL SECOND FLOOR – NIGHT

The elevator door opens. Casi takes Samuel's arm and drags him to the emergency exit door. Nari and Tamarah follow, their guns aimed at the stairwell. An explosion from outside rocks the building. Casi opens the exit door. The alarm sounds. She looks out. The guard comes running over.

GUARD

What happened? Do you need any
help?

CASI

A lunatic downstairs just drew a
gun on us!

GUARD

I'll get him. Hold on.

The guard runs down the hall calling on his radio.
Casi grabs Samuel's hand.

CASI

Tamarah, we will need another car.

TAMARAH

Yes ma'am.

Tamarah hurries out the door. The stairwell door flies open.
Nari fires, hitting the knob and door. Snipes leaps out and
returns several rounds.
Nari dodges.

EXT. STAIRWELL – NIGHT

Casi pulls Samuel down the stairwell. Samuel looks at the getaway car, now
consumed in flames.

SAMUEL

Hold on! I can't move that fast!

Gun fire ERUPTS on the second floor. Casi draws her gun as they reach
the ground.
Nari flies out the emergency exit door, firing her weapon.
She slams the door closed, stands a few seconds with the gun fixed on the
door, then bounds down the steps to Samuel and Casi.

EXT. PARKING LOT—NIGHT

Tamarah hauls up in a sleek black sedan. Casi pushes Samuel into
the back seat.
Samuel glares at Casi.
Nari climbs in, riding shotgun as Tamarah tears away.

INT. SEDAN – NIGHT

TAMARAH

Where to ma'am?

Casi looks at Samuel.

CASI
(*looking at Samuel*)

Where to, Samuel?

SAMUEL

Just take me home.

CASI

Your home? Holmes County? Bad idea.

SAMUEL

I told you my work is done. I need to go home.

Casi sighs and shakes her head.

CASI

(*expressive*)

Samuel. Let me explain this so you'll understand.

SAMUEL

I know what you are going to say. Snipes will chase me down, kidnap my family and likely kill me so he can use the corridor. Right?

CASI

So...let me help you! We need to find your corridor to make sure someone isn't using it.

SAMUEL

Why should I trust you? How do I know you don't want the corridor?

CASI

And have everyone hunting me down? You think I'm crazy? But I don't want my father to have it either.

Samuel looks at her and then looks away for a moment. He sighs.

SAMUEL

All right. It's at Kent State.

EXT. SEDAN -- DAY

We see the Sedan pass through traffic and towns, moving west.
Dozens of military jets zoom in the skies above.

INT. SEDAN – DAY

Tamarah turns on the radio. She plays with the knob until a news brief
comes on.

> NEWSCASTER
>
> ....meanwhile, President Zang, leader of the
> Freedom Force, has consistently denied any
> responsibility for the disappearance of an
> undisclosed number of atomic bombs taken from
> the Arcon Military Plant earlier this morning.
> However, Zang has not commented on his
> involvement in the recent attacks on U.S. military
> bases and troops.
>
> (*pause*)
>
> The whereabouts of the President or his cabinet
> members is still unknown, but sources say the
> President is outraged at yesterday's strike on the
> chain of Arcon plants, and he has sworn to get
> even.

The blood drains from Casi's face.

> CASI
>
> Not again! Not again! That *bastard!*
> Tamarah, take the next exit.

> TAMARAH
>
> Yes ma'am.

Tamara takes Exit 186 at Old Washington, and finds rural Township
Highway 6580. They park in a vacant lot.

CASI

Let's go, Samuel.

EXT. SEDAN -- DAY

Casi leaps out the door and drags Samuel with her.

CASI
(to the cell phone)

Call my father.

Casi pulls out her gun and keeps Samuel next to her.

CASI
(to Samuel)

Stay right there.
(into the phone)
Yes, this is Casi Stone. I need to speak to my father....yes...

Samuel looks at her, wide-eyed.

SAMUEL

Casi, what are you doing?

CASI

Father, yes. It's me. Why are you going to start another war?
(long pause)
Yes, I've got him right here, your hero. But I won't let you get his corridor, YOU...DIRTY... BASTARD!

Casi grabs Samuel's arm.

SAMUEL

Casi...what?

Casi puts her finger to his lips.

CASI
(*to her father*)

You just won't quit!
(*pause*)
I don't care. Now you're on your own.

Casi takes her gun and FIRES three shots into the air.

CASI
(*into the phone*)

Well, that's that.

Casi turns off the phone, looks at Samuel.

CASI

I'm sure that really ticked him off!

SAMUEL

Why did you call him?

CASI

Who cares? With any luck, he thinks you're
dead. Let's go.

*Samuel turns and limps away. Away from the car. Away from Casi and her
bodyguards. Casi catches up with him and takes his arm but he shakes it off.*

CASI

Samuel, wait.

SAMUEL
(*offended*)

Stay. Away. From. Me. You take me out of the
hospital only to call your father? You know we
will be traced!

Samuel turns his back to her and again walks away. Casi keeps up.

CASI

Of course. I'm a walking tracking device.

My cell, my clothes, everything.

> SAMUEL
> (*angry*)

Casi...I don't...

> (*complete control*)

I don't trust you.

He looks at her. She stares back.

EXT. FIELD – DAY

Samuel and Casi sit against a large tree, a little way from the road. Nari and Tamarah wait in the vehicle. Samuel looks angry. Casi looks at her watch and tosses small rocks.

> CASI
>
> Well, I'd give us about another twelve minutes before we're caught.

Samuel shrugs.

> SAMUEL
>
> You. Them. You are all the same.

> CASI
>
> Samuel.

Samuel looks at Casi. Her face reddens and she looks away.

> CASI
>
> I...I have something to tell you. You probably won't believe me, but I swear to you it's true. And please don't laugh.
> (*pause*)
> I can't believe I'm telling you this.

> SAMUEL
>
> What?

CASI

About a year ago I started seeing this face at night...in my dreams. There was nothing else-- just a face. Serious. Sad.
(*pause*)
I never saw that face before and couldn't understand why I kept seeing it.
(*laughs*)
I even went to therapy! I thought I was crazy!

SAMUEL

Why are you telling me this?

CASI

(*quietly*)

Because it was you.

A *beat.*

SAMUEL

(*rolls his eyes but face flushes*)

Me? Right.

CASI

And that's probably the biggest reason why I'm helping you. I *am* trying to help. Samuel, I only want peace, an end to this stupid, mindless mentality of my father. He will use the corridor to fight his enemies, to get even until they are all dead. I don't want him to get it.

SAMUEL

Do you think I want him to get it?

CASI

You don't know him, Samuel. He is...my father is more dangerous than most criminals locked away in prison. He will get revenge on anyone who crosses him, no matter if we're all burned up in a nuclear war.

(*pause*)

Did you know that some top secret jets are
missing? And you heard the radio -- about the
stolen nukes.

SAMUEL

What does that —

CASI

Your corridor. That's the key to all of this.
That's why I can't just let you go off by yourself.

SAMUEL

What? Why not?!

CASI

Because you won't survive
without me.

SAMUEL
(contempt)
Won't survive? I came this far!

Casi moves close to Samuel.

CASI

Snipes will find you.

Samuel rubs the back of his neck.

CASI

Can I offer some advice? Let's find this corridor
and blow it up so no one can ever use it again.

Casi holds up her bag.

CASI

I've got what it takes right here.

SAMUEL
(shakes his head)
I can't do that.

(*quietly*)

I can't do that.

Samuel looks at Casi.

SAMUEL

The corridor is with my sister in Kent.

CASI

Let's go.

INT. SEDAN – DAY

*Samuel looks out the window. Tamarah drives the center lane, north on
Interstate 77.*
*So many vehicles on the road, moving so fast. The huge neon signs give a
harsh, cold world appearance.*
*Video billboards show Samuel and Casi, blown up to a huge size. Captions
beneath the pictures read, "Escaped Criminals, $200,000 reward".*
Samuel looks at Casi, wide-eyed, and sinks down in his seat.

SAMUEL

Didn't they think I was dead?

CASI

Apparently not. Tamarah watch out!

*Tamarah looks to her left to see Snipes, in a futuristic military
Hummer, pointing his gun at her. He fires.*
*Tamarah cries out and wrenches the wheel to the right and ducks. The
bullet blasts through her window and tears into her left shoulder.*

TAMARAH

Aauuuggh!

EXT. SEDAN – DAY

The sedan swerves to the right, cutting off several cars. Then returns to the middle lane. Snipes keeps up. Casi rolls down her window and aims her gun at Snipes.

EXT. SEDAN -- DAY

The Hummer drops behind the sedan.

EXT. HUMMER -- DAY

Snipes fires. Bullets smash out part of the back window.

INT. SEDAN -- DAY

Casi looks at Samuel, who sits low in his seat.

> CASI

Stay down.

> SAMUEL

No problem.

The Hummer swerves into the right lane and drops out of sight. Other cars weave in and out, the DRIVERS desperate to get out of the way.

The Hummer moves forward in the right lane. Snipes fires again, breaking the remaining back window.

Casi and Nari shoot from the car as the sedan swerves. A few bullets hit the Hummer but only glance off. The Hummer moves into the left lane.

Casi takes out four contact plastic explosives.

The Hummer moves up on her left.

SAMUEL

Casi, look out!

INT. HUMMER -- DAY

Snipes aims at her head.

INT. SEDAN – DAY

Casi pulls her head back as a bullet flies past her and takes out Samuel's window. Samuel looks at the window.

SAMUEL

Oh, man. This is getting bad.

Casi hurls the plastic explosives at the Hummer.
One plastic explosive hits the right passenger door of
the Hummer and explodes.
The impact rips the vehicles apart.
The sedan hits the guardrail.
Tamarah grips the steering wheel and steers away from the guardrail. She pales. Blood soaks through her shirt.

CASI
(*to Samuel*)

Thanks.

SAMUEL
(*reddens*)

Welcome.

The Hummer, now with its right door blown off, races the sedan.
Casi aims her gun at Snipes. He pulls the Hummer back. Casi
climbs to the back of the sedan.
Snipes accelerates, aims his gun and fires.
Casi hurls three explosives.
One hits the road, the other two strike the grill of the Hummer and detonate.

The Hummer reels out of control, veers to the right, hits the guard rail and flips high in the air.
Nari takes hold of the steering wheel as Tamarah fades.

NARI

Tamarah, pull over! Pull over now! I'll drive.

CASI (O.S.)
Not yet! We have company!

Nari looks to see five military jeeps overtake the sedan. SOLDIERS fire several rounds and pop two tires. The sedan screeches to an unsteady halt. Jeeps surround the sedan. Soldiers scurry into position.
Casi cocks her 9mm and motions to Nari, who nods. Samuel sinks lower in his seat, his arms protecting his belly.
Two large, jet black, and heavily armed helicopters descend, hovering over the vehicles. They shoot around the soldiers, who dive into their vehicles and back away.
One helicopter shoots a thick gel that strikes the ground and ignites between the sedan and soldiers. Flame and black smoke shoot up. A helicopter lands next to the sedan.

INT. SEDAN – DAY
CASI
Let's go! Out now!

Casi grabs Samuel's arm and pulls him out of the car and into the helicopter.
SAMUEL
Casi. Don't pull so hard!

Nari and Tamarah join them.

EXT. HELICOPTER -- DAY

The helicopter takes off. The second helicopter follows.
From the air we see Snipes crawl out of his wrecked Hummer.

INT. HELICOPTER -- DAY

Casi sits protectively beside Samuel. THOM, early 20's, long hair, glares at Samuel.

> THOM
>
> So this is him? I thought you were going to take him out!

Thom lifts Samuel by his collar, and puts a gun to his head. Samuel stiffens and his eyes widen.

> THOM
>
> Or were you just saving him for me?
> I'll be glad to do it.

Casi grabs Thom by the throat with one hand and pulls his gun away with the other.

> CASI
>
> Leave him alone.

Thom looks at Casi, unbelieving.

> THOM
>
> You said-

> CASI
>
> (*irritated*)
> Yeah, I said. So what? He's not who I thought he was. Let him go! He already took a bullet!

Thom pushes Samuel back down. Casi releases her hold on Thom.

EXT. HELICOPTER -- DAY

Both helicopters buzz over the fields heading north.

TIME CUT:

The helicopters land at an abandoned airfield. Several MEN and WOMEN help unload the passengers.

Eight army Hummers drive up and surround the helicopters.

SOLDIERS jump out and ready their weapons.
Four men shoot smoke grenades at the Hummers. Clouds of white smoke fill the air and the battle begins. Nari pulls Tamarah into the hangar.

Casi and Samuel find a pickup truck and take off.

EXT. ROAD -- DAY

Three Hummers give chase.
Casi weaves the truck back and forth along the dirt road.

INT. PICKUP -- DAY

Samuel holds on for dear life.

> SAMUEL
>
> What's wrong? Want me to drive?

> CASI
> (*pointing*)
>
> Land mines.

Sure enough there they are: small, black and deadly.

> SAMUEL
>
> What —

EXT. DIRT ROAD -- DAY

One Hummer HITS a land mine, explodes and flips over.

INT. PICKUP – DAY

SAMUEL

Oh...

The two Hummers shoot out a scanning ray, detonating the land mines in their path. The Hummers accelerate.

Close in.

Casi looks in the rear-view mirror and shakes her head.

CASI

They won't give it up. Want to drive?

SAMUEL
(*shakes head*)
Hand me your explosives. Time for this to end.

Casi throws him the bag. Samuel pulls out ten.
Casi's eyes widen.

CASI
Whoa, Samuel! What are you—

Samuel slowly climbs out the rear sliding window, and into the bed of the truck. Samuel looks at the soldiers and waves.

SAMUEL

(*shouts*)
Sorry about this!

He opens his hands and drops all ten explosives. We focus on these babies in slow motion until they hit the ground. They erupt, blasting a large crater.
The Hummers fall into the crater.
Casi stops the truck and sticks her head out the window.

CASI

Nice work.

Samuel climbs back in the cab. In the background we see the soldiers climbing out of the hole.

EXT. KATIE'S HOUSE -- DAY

Casi pulls up onto the driveway where a military jeep is also parked. Two SOLDIERS climb out.

INT. TRUCK – DAY

                    CASI
          Don't worry. I'll handle this.

Casi grabs her gun and gets out.

EXT. HOUSE -- DAY
Casi aims her gun at the soldiers. They lift their arms and look at each other in amazement.

                    CASI
          What do you want?

                    SOLDIER
                  (*very nervous*)
          We're here for Samuel Miller.

                    CASI
          Can't have him. Samuel, go!

                    SOLDIER
          But—
                    CASI
          Shut up. Don't say another word.

Samuel runs into the house.
A moment later Samuel comes out with his hat.

SAMUEL

It's not there. Must be at the lab.

CASI

(*to the
soldiers*)

Don't even try to follow.

SOLDIER

(*shakes his
head*)

No, ma'am.

As the truck roars away, one soldier leaps into the jeep and grabs his radio.

SOLDIER

(*excited*)

Commander, we have a problem!

INT. TRUCK, LAB PARKING LOT -- DAY

Katie's Miata is parked. Beside it is Kyle's car.

SAMUEL

Ready?

CASI

(*shakes her head*)

I'll guard out here. Hurry up. You got five minutes.

*Samuel limps to the doors and finds them locked. He knocks.
A large middle-aged MAN appears in the doorway.*

SAMUEL

(*shouting*)

It's me. Samuel Miller.

The door opens and Samuel walks in.

INT. RESEARCH LAB -- DAY

A guard pulls a gun on Samuel and ushers him inside.

GUARD

This way.

Cameron lays on the floor, holding his bleeding side. Hillary kneels by him, holding his hand. Samuel kneels beside Cameron.

SAMUEL
(*alarmed*)

Cam! What happened?!

KYLE (O.S.)

So you came back! Samuel you really are amazing.

Kyle, dressed in a fancy dark suit, is all smiles.

KYLE

Hey, I've made some changes while you were away. Hope you don't mind, though it doesn't matter if you do. We are now in the corridor production business! Automation starts next week!

SAMUEL

WHAT happened to Kyle?

Kyle takes out his 9mm and shows it off.

KYLE

Ain't it a nice one? Oh, sorry. Forgot about your unfortunate upbringing. It came in handy when Cameron...well, let's just say he and I didn't see eye to eye.

SAMUEL
(*shocked*)

You shot your son? Why? How could you shoot your flesh and blood?

KYLE
(*shrugs*)

Actually he's adopted. But let's see. He refused to help build any more corridors. He helped your sister and Jarrod escape to Mexico.
(*to Hillary*)
Get back to work! Still five more to go.
(*to Samuel*)
So what do you think? Is a billion dollars enough to ask for these babies? I've already sold twenty seven! Can you believe it?

SAMUEL
Twenty seven?! Are you crazy?

KYLE
This is just the beginning. And it's all yours Samuel. Well, a good part of it, anyway. Now you can help your family, feed the poor...in fact probably stop world hunger and disease with all the money you'll be making!

SAMUEL
While you help tear apart families? Kill people? Bring the world to the brink of destruction?

KYLE
(*shrugs*)

Let's not play the dramatic card, shall we? Remember, we owed Satellite Systems? I had to pay them off somehow. And hey, I can't control what my clients do with these corridors. I only sell them. I can't help it if they kill the President....take back their countries...

SAMUEL
(grits teeth)
Kill the President?

KYLE

The coward finally showed up at the White
House. We can watch the whole thing on the lab
TV in just a few minutes. What? Why should
you care about him anymore? You did your good
deed and look where it got you! He's not a good
man, Samuel. Not a good man at all.

SAMUEL

So *you* tried to kill him in Iran!

Kyle laughs.

KYLE

Believe me I wanted to, but someone else set that
up. It would have been for the best if you hadn't
interfered. But hey, I don't hold that against you.
So what do you say...help me...make a few
hundred billion dollars...feed hungry people?
(*to Hillary*)
I said, get back to work!

Hillary pulls away from Cameron, whose skin is pale like a sheet.

SAMUEL

We have to get him to a hospital!

KYLE

Um, sorry Samuel. He'd talk, you'd talk, I'd go to
jail. Huh-uh, won't work. Sorry. Anyway, think
about my offer. I'll give you ten minutes. If you
choose to part company, well, you probably have
a good idea what's going to happen.

Kyle leaves. Samuel turns to Cameron.

CAMERON

Sam.

(*coughs
weakly*)

Samuel kneels by Cameron, shaking.

SAMUEL

(*sadly*)

I can't believe he shot you!

CAMERON

I was wrong...about him. I thought he had changed.

(*coughs repeatedly*)

Sorry.

SAMUEL

I have to get you out of here-

GUARD(O.S.)

Don't even think about it.

The man points a gun at Samuel.

SAMUEL

But he's going to die!

The man shrugs.

GUARD

Orders are orders.

KYLE (O.S.)

Hey Samuel, come and watch! This is something you don't want to miss!

The guard motions with his gun.

GUARD

You heard him. Go.

INT. MEETING ROOM – DAY

Samuel and Kyle sit in front of the TV. A live-feed broadcast is underway, outside the Oval Office door. Hundreds of FREEDOM FORCE SOLDIERS and dozens of SECRET SERVICEMEN shoot it out.

KYLE

I have to confess something to you Samuel. I let one corridor go for only half price.

Kyle grins.

KYLE

In exchange for the President. He's a dangerous man. The sooner he's out of the White House, the better. Now we can get the space program up and running again...do some real research.

Samuel stares wide-eyed at Kyle.
An explosion comes from the building entrance, rocking the lab. Rounds of gunfire go off. We hear a loud groan and a heavy thud hit a floor.
Kyle jumps to his feet, gun at the ready.
Casi enters the room, her 9mm pointed at Kyle. He disarms.

CASI

(*really ticked*)

So...Mr. Abraham. A real man of peace? Isn't that Cameron—your own son—who's dying back there?

Kyle shrugs.

KYLE

Hey, what are you getting so ticked about? You said you didn't mind if someone took your father and—

> CASI
> (glances at Samuel)

I do mind.

> KYLE

Since when?

Casi glares at Kyle.

> KYLE

All right, fine. You've turned over a new leaf. But let me show you something before you shoot me, arrest me, or whatever it is you're going to do. Follow please.

Samuel and Katie follow Kyle into the—

INT. POWER CELL PRODUCTION ROOM – DAY

Hundreds of power cell molds are arranged on tables around the room. Several sets of cells are curing.

> KYLE

This is being perfected to a fine art! We complete the molds and program the power cells simultaneously! And they can even activate by remote control. So as you can see, Miss Stone, we have everything we need right here to make us all very rich and determine who rules which part of the world. Join our team and your dreams can come true!

Samuel shakes his head.

> CASI

Wow, you really thought you'd pull this one off? You never learn, do you?

Casi pulls out her cell and dials 9-1-1.

CASI
(*to Samuel*)
Cameron is almost gone.

KYLE
Fine. Have it your way. While the authorities
take their sweet time, I'll just watch the last few
minutes of your father's life on TV. Armies of
our Freedom Force...waging warfare in the Oval
Office...to kill your father.
(*pause*)
But, if you...well, see it my way, I'll call it off.
Your choice.

Casi grabs Kyle by the throat with her gun in his face.
A voice answers her phone. Casi pushed Kyle away and into the
next room while ordering an ambulance.

CASI
(*to Kyle*)
Let's go watch some TV.

INT. CONFERENCE ROOM – DAY

Through the TV we see Freedom Force soldiers smash in the door to the
Oval Office.
KYLE (O.S.)
Going...going...

CASI (O.S.)
Shut up, Kyle. My father can
take care of himself.

Soldiers rush in the room. We hear rounds go off.
Kyle shakes his head at Casi as they continue watching the TV. The camera
moves into the Oval Office, where President Stone stands, surrounded by
three remaining body guards. The President is furious.

PRESIDENT STONE
Not one of you will leave this building alive!

GENERAL ZANG, late 50s, dark with a scarred face, steps forward slowly. He's in charge and isn't afraid to show it. The President sits down in his chair, seething. The General lays a document on his desk.

ZANG
We just destroyed your Pentagon.
(*pause*)
My armies surround the White
House.
(*pause*)
Your 20 generals are on death row.
(*pause*)
But we're *not* going to kill you, Mr. President.

KYLE (O.S.)
What?!

CASI (O.S.)
What?

The President looks at Zang puzzled, then at the document.

ZANG
Killing you would create a martyr. It would not bring peace to our planet. We don't want you dead. We just want you out.

PRESIDENT STONE
Out?! What do you mean, *out?*

President Stone grabs the document and reads it.
He laughs.

PRESIDENT STONE
Every country I have my forces? You expect us to just withdraw? It would mean worldwide chaos in hours! What about the terrorists? How will you maintain the peace? How will you survive?

ZANG

(quiet, dignified)

I have your cabinet members in my custody. Their lives depend on your compliance.

The President sits back in his chair. Zang offers the President a pen. President Stone stares at Zang, looks at the Freedom Force soldiers surrounding him, and shakes his head. He grabs the pen and signs the document.

PRESIDENT STONE

You have condemned us all.

INT. CONFERENCE ROOM -- NIGHT

Kyle stares at the TV, mouth open.

KYLE

That figures. Zang is an idiot after all.

Samuel watches as Kyle takes off in a dead run. Casi pursues. We hear crashing sounds, like metal hitting the floor.

CAMERON (O.S.)

Hurry, Dad! This way to Montana!

Samuel watches as, a few seconds later, Kyle suddenly appears on the TV, inside the Oval Office! Kyle looks bewildered and tries to hide. Freedom Force soldiers bring him to the General.

ZANG

Mr. Abraham?

PRESIDENT STONE

Who is this?

ZANG

The man who sold us the corridors. He paid us to kill you.

The President motions to one of Zang's men. The man grabs Kyle and hauls him away.

> KYLE

Wait! Wait! Mr. President! I have important information about your daughter! She's the *real* terrorist! Not me!

> CASI (O.S.)

Samuel.

INT. POWER CELL PRODUCTION ROOM – NIGHT

Cameron lays on the floor, now by a working corridor. Samuel kneels by his side and takes his arm. We hear the wails of an ambulance in the not too far off distance.

> SAMUEL

Hang on, Cameron. Medics are almost here.

Cameron shakes his head, holds up his hand. He is gasping for breath, fading fast.

> CAMERON

Good trick, huh? I sent my dad...through this corridor...up the river...where he belongs...

Samuel takes his hand and Cameron takes a few big breaths and finally stops. His eyes are raised upward, still.

> SAMUEL

No.

Hillary kneels and cries beside Cameron as Samuel prays.
Samuel looks away trying to fight his own tears.
Casi puts an arm around Samuel's shoulder.

> CASI

I'm sorry, Samuel.

> HILLARY
> (*in tears*)
> Samuel, just before you arrived, I overheard Kyle on the phone arguing with someone named Snipes.

Samuel and Casi look at each other.

> HILLARY
> He's coming for you.

Samuel slowly stands with a determined look.

> SAMUEL
> I need a corridor.

Hillary nods. She disappears and comes back with a briefcase in hand.

> HILLARY
> Take it—ready to go.

Samuel hugs Hillary.

> HILLARY
> (*emotional*)
> I'll see to Cameron.

> SAMUEL
> Please don't let anyone else see those corridors.

> HILLARY
> Done.

Samuel collects a laptop and leaves the lab with Casi.

EXT. PARKING LOT – NIGHT

Samuel and Casi run to the Miata. A light rain falls.

Casi throws her pack and Samuel's belongings in the trunk.

INT. MIATA – NIGHT

Samuel finds the keys behind the visor. He turns on the ignition and stares at the gear controls.

CASI

Where are you going?

SAMUEL

I'm thinking about Canada.

CASI

Let's take it a step at a time. Just get out of Kent first.

TIME CUT:

The car jerks and stalls onto Beryl Drive.
RIOTERS and DEMONSTRATORS throng in the streets, carrying flashlights and weapons.
A police car drives slowly along Beryl Drive. The police car speakers switch on.

POLICEMAN
(filtered)

A curfew is now underway. Anyone found outside their homes will be subject to prosecution.

CASI

What's wrong? Do you want me to drive?

SAMUEL

I'm fine. I just need a little...practice.

CASI

Uh huh. I should have remembered -you're Amish. And still injured. Watch out!

Samuel breaks suddenly as he just misses a pedestrian. A man bangs on the hood of the car. Casi leaps out and opens the driver side door.

CASI

Over.

Casi takes off.
We see a sign: Highway 43: Next Right.
Casi turns onto the Highway.
It rains buckets.

SAMUEL

Still have your explosives?

CASI

In the backpack. Why? Want to blow up Snipes?

SAMUEL

That's tempting. Real tempting.

EXT. HIGHWAY 43 -- NIGHT

A state police car closes in, lights flashing. The
Miata picks up speed.
A helicopter flies over the Miata as rain falls rhythmically from the sky.
The Miata speeds up, and takes the exit onto...

EXT. HIGHWAY 59 -- NIGHT

Two police cars and two military jeeps join pursuit.
Samuel sits low and clings for dear life. Casi laughs as she looks in the rear view mirror.

SAMUEL

Can I drive? Please?

Casi laughs. She is enjoying the chase!

EXT. HIGHWAY 59 – NIGHT

At the junction of Highway 261, two military trucks join the convoy.
Police cars impede the road, 1/2 mile ahead.

INT. MIATA – NIGHT

> CASI
>
> Time for a detour.

She drives the Miata onto Powder Mill Road.
Rain pours. Bigger buckets.
Casi brakes.
The Miata hydroplanes, swerves and plows into a bridge
abutment. The front end is smashed.

INT. MIATA -- NIGHT

The air bags pop open.

> CASI
>
> Are you all right?

Samuel shrugs.
Casi tries to start the car.
It's dead.

> CASI
>
> Any ideas?

Samuel looks through the rear side mirror.

> SAMUEL
>
> A building...back there.

> CASI
>
> Let's go.

Samuel opens his door and looks at the car.

> SAMUEL
> (*stressed*)
> Katie is going to kill me.

He opens the back, grabs his duffel bag and hands Casi her backpack.
Casi supports Samuel as he limps down a small hill. The
helicopter spotlights their every step.
Police and military stop, check the car and run toward the spot light.
Samuel stops to rest. He holds his side in anguish.

> CASI

> Come on Samuel! They're almost here!

Several armed SOLDIERS close in. Casi fires her gun into the air.
The soldiers stop and drop. Bullets fly near Samuel and Casi, and
they drop. The source of the firing: Snipes, away to their left. The
helicopter shines the spotlight over Snipes. Several soldiers block
his way and force him to back off.

The helicopter lands.
Samuel and Casi reach the warehouse. Casi pulls on the old door until
it opens. Soldiers and police follow.

Samuel looks back. Snipes yanks the pilot out of the helicopter.

INT. WAREHOUSE, FIRST FLOOR -- NIGHT

The room is filled with cob webs, old wood beams and decayed siding.
Samuel locks the door.
Casi flips on the light and leads Samuel up to the second floor.

> CASI
> Come on Samuel!

INT. WAREHOUSE, 2ND FLOOR -- NIGHT

Old, creaky, half-rotted steps lead to the third level.
Casi reloads her 9mm. Samuel stops to rest.

We hear the sounds of a door being forced open below.
Casi grabs his hand and they hurry up the stairs.

INT. WAREHOUSE, THIRD FLOOR – NIGHT

Casi turns on the lights where we see a long room. Eight small windows
look to the outside darkness. As they move to the far end, Samuel turns
on his laptop. Casi pulls explosives from her pack.

CASI

I've got the timers.

Samuel carefully places the power cells. Casi sets the timers.
Footsteps sound, many, loud and close.
Samuel looks at Casi. Casi pulls out her gun. Samuel initializes
the corridor.
A dark picture emerges.

CASI

Where is this?

SAMUEL

Near my home.

SOLDIER (O.S.)

Samuel?

Several SOLDIERS slowly approach. Casi aims her gun.

CASI
(*shouts*)

Get out of here! Now!

SAMUEL

Casi! Wait! Put it down!

CASI
(*shakes her head*)

They won't let us go.

(*to the soldiers*)

I said BACK OFF!

Casi fires the gun above her head. A chunk of ceiling falls, revealing a part of the armed helicopter hovering above. The soldiers pause their advancing.

SAMUEL

Casi, don't hurt them!

Samuel steps in front and blocks her aim. Casi glares at him.

CASI

Samuel, go now! I'll take care of the corridor. Don't worry. They won't get it. No one will.

SOLDIER (O.S.)

Samuel!

SAMUEL

(*turns, gasps*)

Daniel?

DANIEL

Samuel!

SAMUEL

Daniel!

As Samuel and Daniel run to each other, the walls are blasted with gunfire. In slow motion we see bullets blowing through the wall just behind Samuel. The soldiers drop.

CASI AND DANIEL

SAMUEL!

Casi and Daniel run to Samuel, still in slow motion. Casi grabs Samuel's legs, narrowly avoiding the bullets. Daniel covers Samuel with his body until the bullets stop.

SAMUEL

Ouch.

CASI

What's the matter? Are you shot?

SAMUEL

No. Daniel's on my ribs. And I'm bleeding again.

The COMMANDER enters. The soldiers stand at attention.
This man wears an army cap that conceals most of his face.
The walls explode with bullet fire. Everyone drops.
The commander walks over to Samuel, who is staring at the floor.
Everything slows down as the man takes his hat off, and for the first time
we see his face: an older version of Samuel.

COMMANDER
Hello little brother!

Samuel eyes reveal it now: instant recognition.

SAMUEL

Amos!

Samuel gingerly hugs his brother, still holding his side.

AMOS
Little brother! You are hard to catch! But we're out
of time. Use your corridor and take the men before
they are killed by that maniac outside. Most of
them are from our community.
(*pause*)
Please.

Bullets strafe the other end of the room.
SAMUEL

Why aren't you coming too?

> AMOS
>
> I have to cover your tracks to throw them off
> your hot trail. I think most of the English world
> is searching for you.

> DANIEL
>
> (*anxious*)
>
> Commander, permission to stay and assist.

Amos holds up his hand to Daniel and shakes his head.
The soldiers line up. Samuel and Casi line up behind them.
Amos searches through Casi's pack. He pulls out a remote device, wire and
explosives. The soldiers salute as they step through the corridor and
disappear. Bullets blast through the walls. Samuel pulls Casi down and
Amos drops.

> AMOS
>
> Samuel! Your computer!

Samuel looks at the laptop, now all shot up. The corridor disappears.

> CASI
>
> Is it...

> SAMUEL
>
> Destroyed.

> AMOS
>
> All right. Plan B. But I need your help.

Amos and Casi take the explosives and attach them to the walls and
rafters. Casi helps Samuel collect the power cells and dead laptop. They
exit to the first floor.

INT. WAREHOUSE, FIRST FLOOR – NIGHT

Samuel and Amos look through a small window near the door.
Several police officers surround the building.

Amos takes a flashlight and searches the room until he pulls a handle on the floor. Up comes a small door. Below are steps. Amos climbs down. Casi and Samuel follow.

EXT. FIELD – NIGHT

Samuel, Casi and Amos crouch in the darkness, hidden by a thicket of bushes. Police remain standing guard.
The helicopter hovers beside the roof, shooting at point blank range. Amos stares at the detonator in his hand.

> AMOS

May God forgive me.

> SAMUEL

Give me that thing!

Samuel grabs the detonator and looks at the helicopter.

> SAMUEL
>
> I don't care anymore.

Amos looks at Samuel in shock. Casi gives him a piercing stare.

> CASI
>
> About time you wised up. What's the big deal?
> He deserves to be blown away.

> AMOS
> (*resigned*)
>
> She's right, Samuel. The first one is always the hardest.

> CASI
>
> The first one is definitely the hardest.

Samuel scrutinizes the detonator. His fist is shaking.

SAMUEL
(*fierce struggle, intense emotion*)
This is stupid. I can do this!

INT. HELICOPTER -- NIGHT

Snipes grins as he fires point blank into the warehouse.

EXT. WAREHOUSE -- NIGHT

The roof collapses.
Bullets detonate the explosives.
The warehouse erupts in a huge ball of fire,
moving quickly toward Snipes.
The helicopter melts in the flames, collapses to the ground and
explodes.
Police yell and run for cover.
Huge flames light up the sky.

EXT. FIELD -- NIGHT

Samuel, Casi and Amos hurry from the blazing warehouse. Samuel starts limping again, as his adrenaline rush starts to die down.

SAMUEL
I-I really wanted to kill him.

Casi places an arm around Samuel's shoulder.

CASI
So did I. It's all right.

AMOS
Let's get you guys home.

EXT. CEMETERY – DAY

It's a bright blue spring day at the Amish cemetery.

Samuel and Casi stand in front of three grave sites: Grandpa Isaac, Grandma Priscilla and Cameron's fresh grave.
Samuel, dressed in Amish attire, holds his hat. He kneels in front of the gravestones. Casi kneels beside him. Tears spill freely from Samuel's eyes.
Samuel gently lays the hat on the grass covering Isaac's grave.

SAMUEL

(*quietly*)

I've come back home, grandma. Just like you said. Just like you wanted me to...

CASI

My mother...she died when I was 13.

SAMUEL

I'm sorry.

CASI

I don't even know why I said that...

Casi picks up the black hat and hands it to Samuel.

CASI

(*gently*)

But there's still more to do, you know? Those corridors. I don't think she would want you to leave your dreams. Not after this.

They stand.

CASI

Come here.

Casi gently hugs Samuel.

SAMUEL

I haven't left my dreams. I saved your father, and

(*sighs*)

... and my work is done.

Casi gently pushes him back and looks deeply into his eyes.

> CASI

Are you sure?

> SAMUEL

I saw everything in my dream fulfilled.

> CASI

I think your real work has only begun.

> SAMUEL
> (*shakes his head*)

I need to be here. My place is here, with my family.

Casi looks at him, disappointed.

> CASI

I spoke with my father this morning.
> (*pause*)

He sounded different. Relieved...somehow. Well, I guess my work here is done.

> SAMUEL

What do you mean? You just got here.

Casi walks away.

> SAMUEL

Casi! Wait...please wait.

Casi stops and turns.

> SAMUEL

If I could use the corridor technology, I would. But I can't and still be a part of this community. I love my Amish life. It's the life I was meant to live.

> CASI

Why did you leave this community if you love it
so much? Was it really because of your dream?
Was it because you were afraid of being drafted?
What...what was it?

Samuel looks into Casi's eyes and then looks away.

> SAMUEL
>
> I had to leave, and now I have to be here. I need
> to be here. In four days I'm going to be baptized.

> CASI
>
> I think you're hiding, Samuel.

Samuel looks at her a moment, then shakes his head.
Casi tears up. She turns and walks away. Samuel's eyes follow her
and tell all.
I want you to be here, too.

INT. SAMUEL'S BEDROOM – DAY

Samuel waits on his bed while his mother removes the last of the wrapping
from his ribs. COUSIN JOHN, 15, assists.

> REBECCA
>
> You can put your shirt back on!

Rebecca looks on with pride. Samuel flushes as he grabs his shirt
and pulls it on. Jacob pokes his head in the door.

> JACOB
>
> Are you finally ready for your baptism, Samuel?

Everyone laughs.

EXT. MILLER HOME – DAY

As everyone climbs into the buggy, Katie's newly remodeled Miata speeds
up the driveway.

Samuel runs to the car.

> SAMUEL
> (*shouts*)
>
> Amos!

They hug and laugh.

> AMOS
>
> Little brother! I heard there was to be a baptism
> today!

*Amos puts his arm around Samuel's shoulders and they walk to the
house. Jacob and Rebecca wave.*

INT. ELDER'S BARN -- DAY

MEMBERS of the Amish community are gathered.
Alfalfa bales are stacked high behind the floor benches where the
WOMEN sit. MEN sit on benches opposite, with two rows in the
middle, where Samuel and eight other AMISH YOUTHS go through the
rites of baptism.

INT. ELDER'S HOUSE -- DAY

The Amish elder stands to his feet and opens his Bible.

> ELDER
>
> Today we are honored to welcome these
> young people into our community.
> (*pause*)
> And our sons are coming home.

The elder removes his hat, looks at it and fingers it for a moment.
Samuel looks at the elder with a steady gaze and a questioning look.

> ELDER
> (*to Samuel*)

Casi Stone asked for our views of this...corridor. She also provided her opinion and her arguments were quite convincing!
(*pause*)
Samuel, the Elders have prayed and argued over this issue for three whole days! We concluded that since Jesus said we are to be witnesses in our communities as well as around the world...
(*pause*)
We believe you have been called into the English world to be such a witness. Moreover, we believe that this invention...this creation that has come forth is of God's design, and we know that God only gives good gifts, perfect gifts. As long as you can help others with this corridor, you are free to travel where you want, as an extension of our community. May the Lord grant you many safe journeys.

The elder shakes Samuel's hand. Samuel grins.
The community members talk excitedly.
Rebecca cries happy tears while Jacob beams proudly. Amos gives a 'thumbs up' sign to Samuel.

EXT. ROAD -- DAY

Skies are clear. The landscape is peaceful. It's a great afternoon. The Miller family ride in their buggy.
Around a corner Casi suddenly appears, standing beside a sedan. The car drives off and Casi motions for a ride.

SAMUEL
Casi! Casi! Father! Please stop!
Jacob pulls the reins on Gabriel.
JACOB
(*welcoming smile*)
Hello, Ms. Stone. Would you care for a ride?

Casi climbs in the back and sits between Samuel and Amos. Samuel's face turns red. Casi pulls out her laptop and turns it on.

CASI

I want you to see this.

The laptop plays a segment from the CNN Morning News.

ANCHOR WOMAN

In yet another surprise move, President Stone has announced a complete reversal in his foreign policies.

The President sits behind his desk in the Oval Office. His demeanor is tired and humbled.

PRESIDENT STONE

Beginning tomorrow, we will withdraw our armed forces from around the world. It has become clear that we can no longer afford the sacrifice of our American soldiers to safeguard the world's depleting oil supplies. We have to move on and apply the new energy strategies available to us. I have also effectively cancelled the draft for all Americans as of yesterday. Those wishing to discontinue their service will be afforded an honorable discharge.

ANCHOR WOMAN

The President also briefed reporters concerning the attack on himself and Secretary of Defense Robert Skiller in Iran four weeks ago.

PRESIDENT STONE

The attack on this Administration stemmed from poor communication between our armed services and my office. We blame no one but our own technology that worked against us and caused great losses to this administration.

The file closes and Casi selects another file.

CASI

And this.

We see videos of the earthquake devastation in and around Mexico City, Mexico. We see a close-up on Katie, Jarrod and Hillary handing out food, clothing and blankets to the local people.

REPORTER

...President Stone has promised to send more aid to assist in the cleanup efforts of this disaster. I'm Dave Pronter for CNN News.

We go back to the anchorwoman.

ANCHOR WOMAN

With the Federal Budget once again in the forefront of politics, President Stone has stated that scientific research is one of the top agendas on his list. Sources say that NASA's Worm-hole studies, once allowed to fall by the wayside, are now thrown into the limelight, and this time with the President's complete support.

CASI

(happy)

He really has changed. This whole ordeal...the assassination attempt, you saving him...I never thought it was possible.

JACOB

With God...all things are possible.

INT. BUGGY -- NIGHT

Skies darken outside but the moon emits a bright glow. Casi looks at Samuel.

CASI

Samuel, I need to talk to you alone. Now.

Samuel looks into her eyes, desiring her.

SAMUEL

Father, mother. Casi and I will walk from here please.

Gabriel stops. Samuel and Casi climb out, and Jacob goes on. Amos waves and winks at Samuel.
Casi takes Samuel's hand and looks at him. He returns her glance. Her face falls.

CASI

Nari and Tamarah are waiting for me...at your house.

(pause)

I'm leaving with them.

Casi stares at Samuel, reading him like a book.
What? Now?

CASI

This is good-bye, Samuel. I have to go back to my father.

I need you.
Casi shakes her head and gently places a finger on his lips.

CASI

I don't belong here.

You belong with me.

CASI
(gently)

You reminded me how important it is to do the right thing, no matter what. I can't hide out here pretending I'm innocent.

What do you mean?

> CASI

Samuel. Oh wow. How do I say this?

> SAMUEL

Honestly.

> CASI

Honestly. Okay.

Casi clears her throat, puts her fingers in the back of Samuel's head and removes the small tracking transmitter. She shows it to him in the moonlight.

> CASI

I sent the order to kill my father. I had given up, I thought there was no other way to stop the wars. I thought I was doing the right thing. I...

Samuel searches her face. Tears cascade down her cheeks.

> CASI

I'll miss you Samuel.

Casi kisses Samuel on the cheek and breaks away. At first a brisk walk, then an all-out run. Samuel stares after her: unbelieving, sad, empty. We see the silhouette of Amos as he walks up to Samuel. The sedan takes off.

> AMOS

Soldiers showed up here today. She didn't want to ruin your baptism so they let her come back and say goodbye.

Amos pats Samuel on the back. Together they walk to the house.

EXT. JACOB MILLER'S HOME -- DAY

Samuel comes out of the house. Daniel sits on the porch steps holding two gloves and a baseball.

SAMUEL

Daniel!

DANIEL
(*quiet*)

Hey Samuel.

SAMUEL

What's up?

Daniel holds up the gloves.

SAMUEL

Hey, your hair is growing back.

DANIEL

Think Katie would like it?

SAMUEL

I do.

DANIEL

So, what about Casi?

Samuel shrugs, sits on the porch beside Daniel.

SAMUEL

I'm over it.

DANIEL

What? Why?

SAMUEL

She's...she's not...

DANIEL
Amish? Neither is Katie. But I don't care anymore.
Come on, let's throw.

They spread out on the yard and Daniel pitches the ball.

EXT. MILLER FRONT YARD – DAY—SIX MONTHS LATER

Falling leaves of many maple trees dance in the wind.
Samuel, wearing his grandpa's hat, sits on a stool and types on a laptop. A wide corridor appears, the size of a barn door.
Amos drives up on a wagon loaded with crates of food. Other Amish
FRIENDS AND NEIGHBORS *drive up in their wagons, also loaded with farm goods. Jacob, Rebecca and John arrive last with newly finished furniture.*
Through the corridor we see a long line of the people Mexico City. Katie and Daniel, hand in hand, stand at the front of the line, waving.

As the wagons line up, a brand new yellow Miata arrives.

Casi gets out and leans against the car for a moment, soaking in all the action. She beams.

Nari and Tamarah pull up behind her in a government sedan.

Everything goes into slow motion as Casi walks toward Samuel.
Samuel's back tenses and slowly turns.
He sees her.
As the wagons pass through the corridor, Samuel runs to Casi.
They embrace and kiss as the...
Credits roll.

FADE OUT:

THE
END

Glossary of Film Terms
Used

Int. –Interior; an indoor location

Ext. –Exterior; an outside location

O.S.—Off–screen; dialogue spoken without seeing the character on–screen

Sotto voce—Spoken at a whisper or under one's breath

About The Author

Bruce Arrington takes your average, everyday characters and upends their lives through unusual and powerful circumstances. His work includes the Josh Anvil series, the Fallen Powers series, the Birthday Wish books, serials like the Phalanx Blood series, and a screenplay such as this one.

Currently Bruce teaches in a small K-12 school, and enjoys challenging students to be their creative best. He writes mostly during the summer, but throughout the year is drawn back into his writing adventures as time allows.

Visit online at www.pipedreambooks.com, https://www.amazon.com/Bruce-Arrington/e/B0064TKY1G, and Facebook at https://www.facebook.com/PipeDreamBooks/.